"Did you come back to town to get even?"

Violet asked.

"Get even for what, Red?" Slow asked.

"You know what. For what happened eleven years ago."

"Why? Is that something you feel guilty about?"

"It's over, Slow," she said ardently. "What happened happened. We can't go back and undo it. Surely you can see that."

"You didn't answer my question."

She sighed. "The answer is *yes.* I feel a little guilty about my behavior then. I promised I'd go with you, and I broke my promise. But I know it was the right decision. It takes more than . . . what we had to make a lasting relationship."

"What do you mean, *what we had?* Come on, Red. Get it out. You can do it," he taunted.

She threw up her hands. "All right. I will. *Sex.* That's what we had. That's *all* we had."

"See, that wasn't so hard, was it?"

Dear Reader,

Welcome to **Silhouette Special Edition** . . . welcome to romance. Each month, **Silhouette Special Edition** publishes six novels with you in mind—stories of love and life, tales that you can identify with—romance with that little "something special" added in.

This month, **Silhouette Special Edition** has some wonderful stories on their way to you. A "delivery" you may want to keep an eye out for is *Navy Baby,* by Debbie Macomber. It's full steam ahead for a delightful story that shouldn't be missed!

Rounding out October are winning tales by more of your favorite authors: Tracy Sinclair, Natalie Bishop, Mary Curtis, Christine Rimmer and Diana Whitney. A good time will be had by all!

In each **Silhouette Special Edition** novel, we're dedicated to bringing you the romances that you dream about—the type of stories that delight as well as bring a tear to the eye. And that's what **Silhouette Special Edition** is all about—special books by special authors for special readers!

I hope you enjoy this book and all of the stories to come.

Sincerely,

Tara Gavin
Senior Editor

CHRISTINE RIMMER
Slow Larkin's Revenge

Silhouette Special Edition

Published by Silhouette Books New York

America's Publisher of Contemporary Romance

For Jesse, who transformed my life

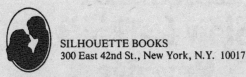

SILHOUETTE BOOKS
300 East 42nd St., New York, N.Y. 10017

SLOW LARKIN'S REVENGE

ISBN: 0-373-09698-4

First Silhouette Books printing October 1991

Printed in the U.S.A.

Books by Christine Rimmer

Silhouette Special Edition

Double Dare #646
Slow Larkin's Revenge #698

Silhouette Desire

No Turning Back #418
Call It Fate #458
Temporary Temptress #602
Hard Luck Lady #640

CHRISTINE RIMMER's

favorite pastimes include playing double-deck pinochle, driving long distances late at night, swimming in cold mountain rivers and eating anything with chocolate in it. She's also a voracious reader and an inveterate romantic daydreamer who's thrilled to have at last found a job that suits her perfectly: writing about the magical and exciting things that happen when two people fall in love. Christine lives in California with her young son, Jesse.

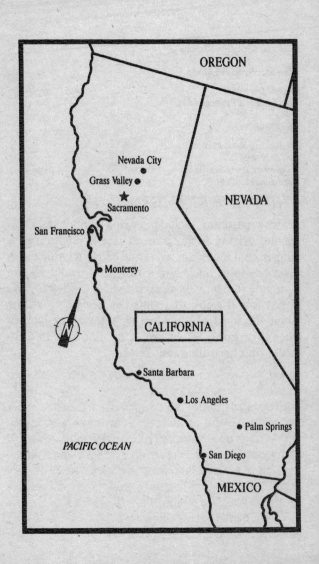

Chapter One

Violet Anne Windemere stood at the parlor window in front of the asparagus fern she'd been misting and clutched her spray bottle in fingers that had gone suddenly numb. Her heart kicked sharply against her ribs. She blinked to clear her sight.

Then she forced herself to look again, through the gauzy lacework of the curtains, and realized that she was indeed seeing just what she thought she had seen: a raven black Chevy Bel Air two-door hardtop in absolutely beautiful condition. A car that a certain boy she'd grown up with would have sold his soul to get his hands on. The driver, invisible in a trick of refracted light on the windshield, was parallel parking the gorgeous thing beyond her own white picket fence, beneath the dappling shade of her linden tree.

With a hand that shook just a little, Violet resettled her glasses on the bridge of her nose.

"Don't be ridiculous, calm down," she told herself in a hissing whisper. "It's only a car. It means nothing. Just because it's a car *he* would have loved doesn't mean it belongs to—"

Her throat closed off the name as the man himself emerged from the car.

Violet's mind spun into chaos. Contradictory snatches of thought assailed her.

It can't be. But it is. Impossible. He looks... older. He looks... the same. And deep down in her heart a triumphant voice cried, *He came, he's here!* while she clutched for composure with the desperation of a woman torn from reality and flung into a bewildering world where dangerous, forbidden dreams suddenly came true.

Violet felt pinned to the gleaming hardwood floor underfoot. She tried frantically to pull herself back into reality again, to tell herself that he wasn't really there.

But he was. After eleven years.

Slow Larkin had returned.

And Violet Anne Windemere quivered from the pure, awful coincidence of his showing up at her front gate on the very day she planned to agree to become another man's wife.

A crafty sunbeam slipped through the shadow of the linden tree to glint off the sunglasses he wore. Behind the black lenses his eyes, like all the years that lay between them, were an enigma to her.

For a moment that seemed to tick on into eternity, he remained on the street side of the car, where he leaned on the roof and appeared to study the house. Then at last he pushed himself away from the car and moved around to the passenger side.

As he came out from behind the car, Violet tore her gaze away from his snake-lean hips and long, hard legs, which were sheathed in snug black denim. Again, nervously, she resettled her glasses on the bridge of her nose. So what if her heart was throbbing like that of a fifties schoolgirl at an Elvis Presley concert? So what if her hands trembled a little, and something down inside her burned and melted at the same time?

It was shock, that was all. The shock of seeing him today of all days after all these years. It would pass, and she would realize that they were little more than strangers now, who had known each other once but had nothing in common anymore.

By rote, Violet finished misting her asparagus fern and set the spray bottle on the old upright piano nearby. Then, still sneaking glances at him through the lacy screen of her grandmother's curtains, she saw the child.

Slow revealed her when he reached the passenger side of the classic car and pulled open the door.

The little girl sat slumped in the seat, her head pointing at the dashboard. Indolently, in an eerily exact copy of the way Slow would have done it, she swiveled her head toward him.

Now that the small face was pointed in her direction, Violet saw a diminutive, feminine replica of Slow. The child had Slow's mouth, with the full lower lip. And his nose, which was a little too big but looked more commanding than anything else. Her hair was lighter than Slow's own dark ash brown—just as Slow's hair had been lighter when he was little.

This feminine Slow-Larkin-in-miniature wore a scaled-down version of Slow's own black-on-black:

black jeans, black T-shirt, black-lensed glasses and black boots.

Violet knew of the child, of course. Violet's mother, Glorianna, who lived in a condo a few miles away, had always adored Slow Larkin and stayed in touch with him over the years. Glorianna invariably kept a current snapshot of Slow's child stuck in the frame of her dressing-table mirror.

"Feast your eyes on that face—on that fabulous *attitude!*" Glorianna Potts Windemere would enthuse whenever Violet gave her half a chance. "Lacy Jay Larkin is just like her father—a rebel and an angel, a lover and a rascal, a darling scoundrel—I can see it in her smile!" Usually at that point Glorianna would sigh deeply. "She should have been yours, my love. Ah, she should have been yours...."

Somehow, though, nine years of listening to Glorianna gush about the daughter Slow had fathered hadn't in any way prepared Violet for the impact of actually *seeing* her in person.

The child swung her legs over the edge of the seat and dropped to the sidewalk. Violet experienced an odd tightness in her chest as father and daughter came through her low white picket gate and began to saunter, side by side, up her front walk.

Suddenly Violet Anne Windemere wanted to cry. She was only thirty-two—much too young to feel all at once so used up and barren. And she was going to marry Darrell and have children of her own. But right then, as Slow and little Lacy Jay mounted her front steps, all she could think of was that bad Slow Larkin had accepted the greatest and most monumental challenge of any life—that of raising a child—and he appeared, in his own inimitable way, to be seeing the challenge through. Even with her law degree and her early partnership in her father's firm, what challenge had Violet ever taken on that could stack up to giving another human being a start in life?

The doorbell rang. Violet, feeling frantic, realized that two fat tears were sliding down her cheeks. She dashed them away, inhaled deeply and counted to ten.

As she counted, the thought occurred to her that she might remain absolutely still; let him ring the bell and knock on the door to his heart's content. Eventually, if she refused to answer, he would have to go away.

But, no—she dragged in another deep breath. Of course she would answer. She was no coward. Whatever had brought Slow Larkin to her door on today of all days, Violet would deal with it head-on.

And besides, it was entirely possible that this visit was a completely innocent one. It had, after all, been such a long time. He'd been married to another woman, and he had a nine-year-old child. Perhaps Slow Larkin now thought of Violet Windemere as no more than someone with whom he'd had a brief fling years and years ago.

Yes, Violet told herself, ignoring the silly pang in her heart at the thought, whatever fanciful imaginings her own mind might have longed to conjure at the sight of him, the truth was surely more mundane.

Probably they were simply looking for Glorianna. In the occasional letters and phone calls that Glorianna and Slow shared, Slow had promised more than once that some day he'd return and pay Violet's mother a visit. Most likely they'd already dropped in at the condo and Glorianna hadn't been there. It would be only logical that they would try the Windemere house next, where Violet now lived alone.

The doorbell rang again. Violet, positive now that she had the situation figured out, steeled herself to answer.

There would be no more hesitation—not even for the briefest of glances in the mirror above the sofa. She knew exactly how she looked anyway. She was wearing old cutoff jeans and a wrinkled shirt. Her slightly freckled face, which needed all the cosmetic help it could get, was scrubbed clean of makeup. Her red hair lay squashed beneath an ugly scarf.

And there was nothing wrong with that, she reminded herself. Her appearance was completely appropriate for a woman who had been puttering around her house on a Saturday afternoon. She wasn't some giddy schoolgirl who needed to rush to the powder room before she'd open the front door on the only man she'd ever known intimately, whom she hadn't seen in eleven years . . .

"Oh, my God," she groaned aloud as the doorbell rang for the third time. On legs that felt disconnected from her body, Violet forced herself to move. The walk across the tastefully faded Oriental rug to the arch that opened on the front hall seemed to take half a lifetime, but Violet accomplished it.

Too soon, she stood beneath the globe-and-cast-iron ceiling fixture in the hall, gazing blindly out through the panes of etched glass that graced the top half of the double front door. Then just as the bell rang for the fourth time, Violet opened the door.

After that, she had no idea what to do next. She stood there, the banalities that her good manners prompted her to utter dying on her tongue. Two pairs of dark glasses watched her.

At last Lacy Jay said, elbowing her father, "She's not smiling, Dad. You better say something, or I get the feeling we're outta here."

Somehow the sound of Lacy Jay's voice loosened the constriction in Violet's throat. She found, astonishingly, that she could speak. So she said, "Excuse me. You've surprised me, that's all. I wasn't expecting...company today."

Lacy Jay grinned, displaying white, even teeth like her father's. "'Specially not us, I bet."

"Yes, well. I suppose you could say that."

"I'm Lacy Jay." The child grinned wider and held out a hand with black polish on the slightly chewed-looking nails. Violet gave the hand a brief shake, thinking how small and vulnerable it felt within her own. "And this is my dad—but you know him already, right?"

"Yes." Violet, wondering how much the child had been told, forced herself to look directly at Slow. She murmured, "Hello, Slow," and even managed a prim facsimile of a smile.

Slow Larkin raised an arm and casually removed his dark glasses. With a lurch in her stomach that was part thrill and part dread, Violet came to grips with the fact that his eyes were still blue. Deep blue. To-drown-in blue. Dangerous blue...

"'Lo, Red," Slow drawled.

His taunting smile, coupled with the use of the nickname that only he had ever dared to call her, made her doubt once again that his motives for being on her doorstep could possibly be innocuous. She'd been on the verge of asking them in, but now caution advised against such a move.

Violet asked civilly, "What can I do for you? Are you looking for Mother? You did try the condo, didn't you?"

"Not yet."

"Oh?" Violet asked on a raising inflection and then paused so that he might explain what he meant.

All he said was "We wanted to get settled in first."

"Excuse me?"

"You heard me." His blue gaze began a leisurely pass down to her canvas shoes and back up again.

"Settled in? Oh, you mean you're staying in town for a while?" Her voice came out brittle. Her strained politeness was beginning to fray at the edges.

"Yeah. A long while," he said once his eyes had finished taking a walk all over her.

Violet felt her temper rising. He was no different than he'd ever been: rude and pointlessly mysterious, looking her over with insinuating eyes and making a guessing game out of what needn't have been more than a courteous exchange of information.

"Dad," Lacy Jay piped in then, "I don't think Glorianna told her, y'know?"

"Told me what?" Violet asked, feeling dread, on cold little feet, skittering up her spine.

Slow pulled a key from his pocket and handed it to Lacy Jay. "Go on and get the stuff from the trunk," he said.

"Right," Lacy Jay answered with a shrug worthy of the man who had fathered her. Then she turned for the car.

Violet, once again assailed by dizzying sensations of unreality, said nothing until the child was halfway down the walk.

She used his full name when she spoke, hoping that would make him realize how serious she was. "*Winslow* Larkin, what is going on here?"

Once again Slow smiled his bad-boy smile. "Lacy Jay and I are coming home," he said.

Violet swallowed. "Here? To Nevada City?"

He nodded.

"For good?"

"That's right."

Violet's feelings of unreality increased. This couldn't really be happening, her mind kept protesting. Somehow, while misting her asparagus fern, she'd fallen down an emotional rabbit hole into a world where everything was backward and the impossible was coming to pass. As a result, she now found herself standing on her front porch listening to Slow Larkin tell her that he was moving back to Nevada City. To stay.

"But you despise Nevada City," she heard herself protesting in a desperate voice. "You always have."

His expression was unreadable. "It's been a lot of years, Red. Maybe I've changed. Did you ever think of that?"

She made a scoffing sound. "I don't believe it. You're up to something."

Slow's face grew hard and he glared at her. "Yeah, I am. I'm after a fresh start for my kid in a place where it's safe for her to walk home from school alone. You got an objection to that?"

Violet said nothing for a moment as his words sunk in. Then she answered honestly. "No, Slow. No objection. There's nothing wrong with that."

"All right, then," he said, his voice gruff but his expression less hard. They stared at each other for endless seconds, then Violet forced herself to break the hold of his gaze.

She looked beyond him to the street where Lacy Jay was raising the trunk of the Chevy. Violet watched as the child hoisted out several black duffel bags and turned to drop them on the concrete sidewalk nearby.

She turned again to look Slow in the eye. "You can't really be thinking of staying here, in my house..." Her voice lost conviction and faded off as she read in his eyes that he intended to do precisely that.

He said, "This house still belongs to Glorianna, doesn't it?"

"That doesn't matter," she shot back tartly. "*I'm* the one who lives here."

"But she *does* own it."

Violet looked away, deciding not to argue about a silly issue like that. A charged silence thickened the balmy late-summer air as Violet regathered her determination. When she looked back at him and spoke again, it was with all the authority and firmness she possessed.

"No, Slow," she told him. "Absolutely not. Tell Lacy Jay to put the bags back in the trunk."

He shook his head—slowly, of course. "Sorry, Red. Glorianna invited us to stay. She offered us the use of the upstairs while we look for a place of our own. We're moving in with you for a while. If you have a problem with that, take it up with your mother."

Chapter Two

Violet became aware of a queasy, trapped feeling in her stomach as Slow's words sunk in. Unfortunately she held out little hope that Slow might be lying. Glorianna, after all, practically worshiped at Slow Larkin's feet. She wouldn't have hesitated for a second to offer him a place in the house—whatever Violet might think of the idea.

And the house, legally at least, did belong to Glorianna.

Grudgingly Violet admitted the weakness of her own position. In the end, her options were few. She might shut the door in his face now, only to have to let him in later if she couldn't convince her mother to retract her invitation.

As Violet hesitated over whether or not to go ahead and shut the door anyway, Lacy Jay came bumping back through the gate. Gamely the small girl dragged a big bag in each fist. Huffing and puffing, she forged up the walk and then started up the steps. Without even thinking about it, Violet instinctively moved forward to help lighten the load. But before she could step beyond the threshold, Slow put a hand on her arm.

"Let her do it herself," he said quietly. "She's an independent kind of kid."

Violet froze, stunned at knowing again the warmth of his touch. It struck her anew how impossible it was that he was actually here. She blinked, and when she opened her eyes again her bewildered gaze drifted to his lips. She wondered if, like the touch of his hand, his kiss would feel the same as before.

It was a question, she told herself firmly, to which she would never know the answer. As casually as she could, not wanting either the man or the child to realize how much a simple touch affected her, Violet pulled her arm free.

Slow let go without resistance, looking a little stunned himself.

Lacy Jay negotiated the last step and dragged the bags the final eight feet to the front door. "There," she announced proudly, letting go of the bags. "Two down, four to go." Lacy Jay shoved her dark glasses up into her bangs. The shining eyes the action revealed were dark hazel—a detail Violet had never really absorbed from looking at Glorianna's snapshots. Somehow she'd always assumed that the child would have blue eyes like Slow's.

The fact that Lacy's eyes were *not* Slow's eyes brought home to Violet that the child was much more than an extension of her father. And as Lacy Jay grinned up at her, Violet perceived that while she might be thoroughly capable of shutting her door in Slow Larkin's face, closing it on an innocent—and thoroughly appealing—child was another story altogether.

She came to a decision. She would let Slow and his daughter into the house, allow them to stay the night. And as soon as she'd seen them settled in, she'd get over to her mother's condo and insist Glorianna retract her totally unacceptable invitation.

Violet stepped around Slow, who was still staring at her rather strangely. She hoisted the two duffel bags, one in each fist.

"Don't just stand there," she said to Slow. "Help Lacy Jay get the rest of your bags and then follow me upstairs." With that, she turned and marched resolutely into the house.

Upstairs there were two baths and four bedrooms. Violet assigned Slow the master suite, valiantly closing her mind to images of her father, dressed in the fine gabardine suit he'd been buried in, writhing in his grave. Clovis Windemere III would not have taken kindly to the news that bad Slow Larkin would be spending the night in his bed.

However, Violet wanted zero dissension with Slow, so she intended to give him absolutely no cause to argue with her. He certainly couldn't complain if she gave him the best room in the house—looming four-poster, mahogany serpentine chests and all.

Slow managed to catch her eye as she signaled him into the huge room. "You could use a new rug in here," he muttered dryly.

She had to resist the urge to inform him that the carpet looked old because it was an antique. And then she was glad she'd kept her mouth shut, because his sly grin told her he knew very well that the carpet was valuable.

He'd hinted out on the porch that he had changed. If he had, she'd yet to see how. He still dressed like a delinquent, drove an old car and couldn't open his mouth without something rude coming out.

Showing no reluctance to treat Violet's home as his own, Slow flung his duffel bags on a love seat and himself down on the bed. He began pulling off his boots. "Over four hundred miles I drove today, Red, mostly on Highway 5." The interstate that ran down the center of California was a rough one to drive—not because of the road itself, but because of its lack of visual interest; it tended to put motorists to sleep. "From North Hollywood to my hometown, in nine hours that seemed like a lifetime," Slow continued. "Is there a more boring piece of asphalt in this country? Let me know if there is so I can avoid it." Slow stretched luxuriously and fell back on the pillows with a lusty sigh.

"Just make yourself comfortable," Violet remarked sourly.

"Thanks, I will. God, I'm beat."

"Take a nap, then." Violet turned toward the door to the hall.

"Red?" Slow's voice, grown suddenly husky, stopped her in midstride.

"What?" Though she knew she shouldn't, she glanced back at him. A few strands of thick hair had escaped the rest and fallen across his forehead in a teasing question mark that kissed the center of his brow right above his nose. The effect was devastatingly delinquent.

"Where are you running off to?" he asked, his brow furrowing slightly beneath the question mark of hair.

"To find your daughter and make sure she's settled in—is that all right with you?"

"Could you . . . pull the curtains before you go?"

Violet gave him her best blood-freezing smile, the kind she reserved for clients who lied to her, or family members who bickered at the reading of a will. "Absolutely, Slow," she replied and went around the big room shutting out the bright afternoon light. "Is that better?" she asked when she was done.

"Much."

"Anything else?"

He laced his hands behind his head, sleek biceps flexing with the action, and crossed his stocking feet. "What's for dinner?"

"Why, whatever you want, I imagine. It's totally up to you. *I'm* going out."

He lifted an eyebrow at her. "Don't tell me. With Straight-Arrow Darrell."

"Slow, you are a grown man," Violet reprimanded him, her voice tart as a schoolteacher giving a dressing down to a recalcitrant student. "I would think you would have gotten beyond the need to call other people childish names by now."

He shrugged. "I'm just bad, Red. I've always been bad." His voice had become husky again. He was blatantly mocking her, she was sure of it now—taunting her with just how bad he could be and how much she had once liked it. Then he grinned and chuckled. "And Darrell will always be a straight arrow to me."

Violet didn't bother to reprimand him again, because she could see it would do no good. He seemed to be stirring up trouble purely for the fun of it—just as he used to do when they were children, when making waves had been his primary mode of operation.

Their fathers—Slow's, her own and Darrell's—had worked side by side as partners in their law firm of Larkin, Windemere and Carruthers. All three children, each an only child, had been destined from the first to lead successful, settled lives doing exactly what their fathers had done before them.

But Slow had always refused to fit the mold. He'd been in trouble before he was out of diapers, pulling stunts like shoving Violet in the fish pond out back and knocking out two of Darrell's baby teeth with a toy hoe. As a boy, he was inevitably the one who wandered off dressed in his Sunday best to catch frogs down in nearby Gold Run Creek.

Then as he grew into his teens, instead of working like mad to get into Stanford the way Darrell and Violet were doing, Slow had begun his lifelong, all-consuming love affair with the internal combustion engine.

It had always been cars, cars and more cars to Slow Larkin. It was a car that had gotten him run out of town when he was eighteen, and cars that eventually made him his fortune. His company, Classic Cars, Incorporated, which rebuilt and restored old cars down in Southern California, was doing a bang-up business—at least according to the articles about it in magazines like *Car and Driver* and *Road and Track,* articles that Glorianna always managed to clip and leave lying around for Violet to read.

On the bed, Slow chuckled. "What are you thinking about, Red?"

"Nothing that concerns you." She told the lie without remorse and reminded herself that she was supposed to be out the door by now. But deep-set eyes were casually studying her legs, and somehow she found herself unable to move as her skin warmed in a slow-spreading, too-pleasurable flush.

"You know, you've still got the best legs in Nevada County." Slow's lazy drawl insinuated its way under her skin. His gaze wandered upward to her face. "And you're still hiding behind your glasses, just like you always did. But that's okay, really. In a way, I always liked your glasses. Do you want me to tell you why?" The right corner of his mouth quirked, a promise of a smile that he didn't quite deliver.

Violet pressed her own lips together. She was not, under any circumstances, going to ask him what he liked about her glasses. She was going to turn, right now, and march out the door.

"Hey, it's okay!" he exclaimed when she neither moved nor spoke. "You don't have to beg me. I'll tell you."

"I really couldn't care less," she announced with a coolness she was far from feeling. "And I have to go find your daughter now."

Before she could take a step, he told her anyway. "I like your glasses because once I get them off you you do the *damnedest* things..."

Quickly, before he could go into detail, Violet turned and fled the room. His deep, lazy laugh followed her out into the hall. But at least he himself stayed where he was.

Blocking out the thought of him, Violet went looking for Lacy Jay. She found her without having to go downstairs, in what had been the maid's room when

Violet's grandmother ran the house—a small, angular space tucked up in the north corner of the second floor.

In the room, Lacy Jay was sitting on the old iron-framed bed, her duffel bags forgotten on the rag rug at her feet. She was staring out the single small window that overlooked the backyard and a section of Cottage Street. She turned her head as Violet came through the door.

"It's kind of weird. I mean, here we are," Lacy Jay said. For the first time in her brief acquaintance with the child, Violet detected a note of sadness.

The view that the small window framed was lovely: a section of green lawn, a tree-shaded street and pine-covered hills in the distance. But Violet understood that the beauty beyond the window was not the issue for Lacy Jay. Lacy Jay was thinking about home. "You're missing Southern California?" Violet asked.

Lacy Jay shrugged. "I guess. We always lived in North Hollywood, since I was little. My mother always wanted to move someplace nicer, but Dad always said you weren't alive unless you wondered every day if you might get mugged." Violet blinked in surprise at that and thought about what Slow had said on the front porch, about wanting a safer place to raise Lacy Jay. Lacy Jay must have read Violet's expression, because she quickly jumped to her father's defense. "Don't think my dad thinks getting mugged is a good thing. To be on your toes, that's what he means. Not to get like most people, half-dead from their lives always being just the same every day."

"I see," Violet said and decided it would be unwise to say more.

"You got to get to know my dad to understand the things he says," Lacy Jay added.

"I'm sure."

Lacy Jay turned her head and looked back out the window. "But all of a sudden we're living here now." Violet thought that Lacy Jay was as confused by the move as she was herself.

"Give it time," Violet advised. "You might end up liking it here."

Lacy Jay considered that idea. "I guess." Then she smiled. "You got a fish pond out there. Lily pads and everything."

"Yes, and goldfish, too. It's been there as long as I can remember. My grandfather had it put in, I believe."

"Yeah, my dad pushed you into it once, huh?"

Violet was surprised. "How did you know that?"

"My dad told me. He told me lots about you."

"He did?" Violet knew she shouldn't ask, but she couldn't help it. "Like what?"

"Oh, like that you're smart and you have a hard, good job. And things you did when you were kids. Stuff like that." Lacy Jay was looking back out the window again, and Violet allowed herself a smile, pleased in spite of herself that Slow had spoken of her, in apparently friendly terms, to his daughter. Then Lacy asked, "Can I stay in this room, for as long as we're here?"

"Sure." Violet had planned to give her the much larger and brighter east bedroom opposite the master suite, but she understood the special appeal of this particular room. It seemed scaled to the needs of a child, especially one who was a little bit homesick for the life she'd left behind. The scarred straight-backed chairs and the battered chest of drawers would be like old friends in a new place, comforting and familiar right from the first. And the cozy proportions of the room itself would reassure her if she woke in the night and wondered where she was.

"Thanks," Lacy Jay said. "I like this room."

"I'm glad—and you're welcome."

It was going to be nice, Violet decided, to have Lacy Jay in the house—and then she caught herself up short before her thoughts went any further.

She had to remember that along with this engaging little girl came Slow Larkin—and with Slow Larkin came *trouble*. If Violet had anything at all to say about it, Lacy Jay and Slow would be checking in at a hotel within the next twenty-four hours.

In fact—Violet glanced at her watch—it was near four o'clock, and if she wanted to have it out with her mother and still be back in time to dress for dinner with Darrell, she had better get a move on.

"Come on." Violet tilted her head toward the stairs. "I need to leave in a few minutes. I'll show you the kitchen and pantry, in case you want to find something to eat while I'm gone."

Lacy Jay's smooth brows drew together. "Where are you going?"

"To... talk to my mother," Violet answered, and then waited grimly for the child to ask why.

But Lacy only said, "Oh." She jumped off the bed, ready to follow Violet down the stairs.

In the butler's pantry, Lacy giggled over the dumbwaiter that provided easy access to the stone cellar below. Then she obediently listened to Violet's advice about the operation of the new microwave that sat on a counter in the kitchen. She was assembling the ingredients for tuna sandwiches for herself and her father when Violet left her to slip into a presentable pair of slacks and run a quick comb through her hair.

Violet's bedroom, off the kitchen, was furnished in simpler style than the big rooms upstairs. It had its own door to the downstairs bath and had been added on to the house during the great depression for an unmarried great-aunt who had lived in it until her death, before Violet was born. Violet had taken the room when she moved back into the house during her father's final illness a few years ago. After her father's death, she had remained in the room because she found it easier, living alone as she did, to keep to the first floor.

When Violet ventured once more into the kitchen, she found that Lacy Jay had already gone upstairs.

She left through the back service porch. Her nice, practical car waited in the woodshed, which had become the garage in the thirties when the Queen Anne-Gothic house was converted to gas heat.

Violet was behind the wheel and backing out onto Cottage Street in the blink of an eye. She turned left at the corner and within a hundred yards down the road East Broad became central Broad. She drove through the heart of Nevada City's Gold Rush Victorian historical district, hardly noticing its considerable nostalgic charm. At the base of Broad, just past the heavily corniced facade of the grand old National Hotel, she swung onto the entrance of the relatively new superhighway that linked Nevada City with her larger sister, Grass Valley.

It took ten minutes for her to arrive at the attractively landscaped guest parking area of Towering Pines, a huge condominium complex that Glorianna

Potts Windemere now called home. Eager to get the confrontation over with, Violet fairly bounded up the steps to her mother's second-floor residence.

"Violet Anne, how lovely!" The artful color on Glorianna's cheeks deepened with real pleasure when she flung her door wide and found Violet standing there.

"Hello, Mother."

Glorianna threw her arms wide and Violet found herself engulfed in the folds of the black silk kimono she wore.

With her cheek against her mother's, Violet allowed herself a smile. She felt the springy pressure of her mother's hair, so much like her own, except that now Glorianna required a little help from a bottle every six weeks to keep it as brashly red as Violet's managed to be naturally.

Glorianna stepped back and gestured widely with a plump arm. "Come in, come in." She swept ahead of Violet down the narrow hall, and the red dragon rearing on the back of her kimono seemed to lunge and subside with each step she took.

They went into the living room, a tall, skylit space furnished in a style that, to Violet, always brought to mind images of what a Shanghai bordello must look like. There were black lacquer tables, shell-inlaid chests and lots of prints of exotic birds framed in gold bamboo. The lamps all sported rice-paper shades watercolored with pagodas. The carpet was red and black, and the heavily padded armchairs and couch were upholstered in red velvet. Sandalwood incense smoked on the black marble mantel.

"Oolong? Soda pop? Scotch and water?" Glorianna recited with feeling as she flung out an arm toward the modular couch, which embraced a low lacquer table. Until her fortieth birthday, when she married Clovis Windemere, Glorianna Potts had been a stage actress. Though thirty-five years had passed since she'd trod the boards, Glorianna could still make offering a beverage into a theatrical event.

"Nothing, just your attention," Violet said, her voice brisk. She took a seat on the couch and, with a quick, no-nonsense motion, set her shoulder bag on the low table in front of her.

"Uh-oh!" Only Glorianna Potts Windemere could make *uh-oh* sound like the end of the world. "What have I done now?"

"Would you sit down, Mother? And relax. I just want to...ask you something."

Dramatically Glorianna swooped to a section of couch at a right angle to her daughter and draped an arm along the velvet backrest. "What is it, my love? Ask away."

"Mother, did you invite Slow Larkin to stay at the house?"

Glorianna's eyes widened beneath their sweeping false lashes. "He actually *came?* He's actually *here?*"

"You did, then?"

Glorianna soared from her seat. "Oh, my angels in heaven, isn't it fabulous? Slow Larkin has returned to us at last!"

Violet rubbed at her temples. "Mother, you had no right—"

"Oh, but of course I had the right, darling. The house belongs to me, remember? And it's too big for you all by your lonesome anyway." She swooped to pat Violet on the cheek and then stood tall again to pace the room in leonine strides and embark on one of her endless extemporaneous orations.

"He's brought Lacy Jay, hasn't he? Oh, good. We are going to have such fun! I can hardly control myself—I must get Arthur on the phone immediately." Arthur was Glorianna's latest amour, a "younger" man of sixty-two whom she'd met at a square dance in Auburn six months before.

Violet smoothly rose and depressed the disconnect button on the phone Glorianna had already begun dialing. Glorianna lifted sculpted brows and granted her only child a smile full of artful innocence. "Don't be a spoilsport, my love. You know how I adore that boy. Humor your poor old mother, just this once. *Please...*"

"You're only old when it's convenient, and I do not want him staying in my house."

"*My* house, my love."

"You've always hated that house. You offered to sign it over to me when you learned Father had left it to you."

"Yes." Glorianna's smile turned to a self-satisfied smirk. "But you wouldn't hear of such a thing. You said, 'Mother, I'll get it anyway someday, and until then I insist on paying rent.' But then, of course, I couldn't have allowed my own daughter to pay me to live in her father's house, could I? So here we are, with you staying in *my* house and me completely within my rights to invite a guest or two to visit now and then."

"Mother, I will go crazy if that man stays in my house."

"*My* house." Glorianna's smile went from smirking to sly. "But why will you go crazy?"

"Because he..." Violet almost said something thoroughly incriminating, but stopped herself in time. She finished by muttering insipidly, "He's always making trouble."

"That's not what you were going to say," Glorianna accused.

"Never mind what I was going to say."

"If you're going to go crazy, you can at least tell me the real reason why." Glorianna batted her false eyelashes and assumed a pleading air.

"Mother." Violet glared. "Drop it. Now."

"Oh, but I can't, my love. Let there be honesty, at least between us. If you won't come out and say it, then allow *me* to explicate."

"Drop it, Mother," Violet reiterated. The order was cold as ice. In a court of law, even opposing council sat up and took notice when Violet Windemere used such a tone.

But it didn't faze Glorianna in the least. She continued. "The real reason you think you'll go crazy if Slow stays in your house is because he still *excites* you—"

"That's ridiculous, Mother," Violet interjected, sounding disgustingly defensive.

"*And* because you've never forgotten that you were once in love—"

"We were kids, Mother."

"*And* because you threw him over and you've always known deep down that you made a terrible mistake—"

"I did *not* throw him over."

"Ah, the lies we tell ourselves," Glorianna chanted in an infuriating little singsong.

"Mother!" Violet clutched mentally for composure and somehow found it.

"Yes, my love."

"Please just tell him that you made a mistake and you realize now that you never should have offered the use of a house that isn't really yours."

"But it *is* mine."

"Get him a room at a hotel until he's found something else. Look, I'll even pay for it—"

Glorianna nobly intoned, "One doesn't open one's doors to a dear friend on one day and then ask him to leave the next."

"He's *not* my friend."

"No, he's mine. What he is to you, you refuse to face."

Violet felt her defensiveness growing again—and fought it by going on the attack. "I don't refuse to face anything. You're the one who lives in a fantasy world about this whole situation."

"Oh, do I?"

"This is my *life,* Mother, not *Hello Dolly!*—"

"Well, I know that, dear."

"And your matchmaking has got to stop!"

Glorianna's seventy-five year-old face looked innocent as a baby's. "Why, sweetheart, I never—"

Violet didn't allow her to finish. "I'm marrying Darrell, Mother. That's reality and you'd better get used to it. Your little plot to throw Slow and me together isn't going to accomplish a single thing but *trouble* for everyone involved."

Glorianna was now looking grievously injured. "I'll have you know there was no plot. No plot whatsoever, and that is the absolute truth."

"Oh, come on, Mother. Don't treat me like an idiot. I know very well that you called Slow the minute I told you that I planned to marry Darrell, and you *lured* him up here with Lord knows what fantastic stories."

Glorianna was shaking her mane of red hair. "Slow Larkin is not the kind of man who can be lured. You should at least realize that much about him."

"You're telling me you didn't call him?" Violet challenged.

Glorianna didn't hesitate. "That is precisely what I'm telling you. *He* called *me*. He does every month or two, you know."

"And?"

Glorianna rolled her eyes. "What do you want, a blow-by-blow dissertation?"

"Yes. Tell me what was said."

"Oh, all right."

"I'm listening."

"Fine. Yes, I mentioned—*only* mentioned—that you had decided to marry Darrell. And then he told me that since Loni's death he's begun thinking it might be a good idea to give Lacy Jay a chance at a different sort of life."

Violet looked away. What her mother said was the same as what Slow had told her while she held him at bay on her front porch. And it made complete sense. What caring father wouldn't want the best possible start in life for his only child?

"He told you that same thing, didn't he, that he's moving here because of Lacy Jay?" Glorianna prodded, sounding smug.

Violet swung back to face her mother. "Go on."

"There isn't much more."

"Except that you invited him to stay with me until he found a place."

"Yes, I did." Glorianna raised her proud nose high. "And I fully intend to stick to my word."

"Mother, you have no right—"

Glorianna hid a yawn behind her plump hand. "Ah, we're back around to 'rights' again, are we? You sound just like that darling old prig who fathered you, and you know how far Clovis's relentless self-righteousness got with me!" Glorianna alluded to the fact that she had finally left Clovis, swearing never to return, when Violet was in college—though in the end she *had* come back when Clovis became terminally ill and, with Violet's help, had nursed him until he died.

Violet, forcing her mind to remain on the issue at hand, declared, "If you think I'm going to meekly sit by while Slow Larkin takes over my house—"

The sound of the door chimes cut Violet off.

Glorianna looked massively relieved. "Ah, more company. At times it's a strain to be so popular. Why don't you wander on into the kitchen? Pour yourself a nice, stiff drink—and one for me, too. Scotch will do fine. I'll see who it is."

"Mother, this conversation is not concluded yet."

Glorianna was already striding toward the hall. "Yes, well, we'll see about that. But right now there's someone at the door."

Violet resisted the urge to subside against the velvet sectional and stood as her mother's kimono sailed out of sight. She knew she mustn't let herself relax until she'd convinced Glorianna to concede to her demands. She decided she'd go ahead and mix the drinks. However she'd barely edged around the lacquer coffee table when she heard the exultant shout from the front door.

"Slow! Lacy Jay!" her mother roared in the stage voice that had never, no matter how big the hall, required a microphone. "I simply cannot believe it, you're here at last!"

Damn him! He had tracked her down. What now? Violet hadn't a clue, and so she kept moving until she could figure out what to do next. She slid around the couch and beat a path to the other hall and the kitchen at the end of it.

In the kitchen, which was mostly purple because Glorianna considered purple a color of great power, Violet mixed the drinks. When she'd poured them, she took one firmly in each hand and marched back down the hall.

In the living room again, she found Glorianna pacing grandiosely. Slow was sprawled in a red velvet recliner, and Lacy Jay had perched on an arm of the sectional sofa.

"There you are!" Glorianna exclaimed, as if Violet had been missing for years. "Oh, and you've poured my Scotch, too. How thoughtful of you, my love." She held out her hand and Violet gave her the glass. Glorianna sipped. "Heavenly—Slow, Lacy Jay? What can we get for you?"

"I'm sure they can't stay but a minute," Violet muttered, casting a murderous look in Slow's direction.

In the huge red chair, Slow, who had been staring at Violet with an irritating smirk on his face since she'd entered the room, said, "Oh, we can stay all right. At least as long as *you* can, Red—but I'm not really thirsty right now. I had a can of soda with the sandwich Lacy Jay made me at your house."

"And you, Lacy Jay?" Glorianna asked.

"A root beer, I guess. If you've got one."

"Certainly I have one. Follow me." Glorianna sailed out of the room in the direction of the kitchen. Lacy Jay followed.

Somehow, though it wasn't supposed to happen, Violet found herself alone with Slow Larkin—again. She glanced desperately around the room, looking everywhere but at him. Then, since she had it right there in her hand, she knocked back a slug of the Scotch, hoping it might give her strength. The sudden heat of it closed up her throat and she started coughing.

"You okay, Red?" Slow asked from across the room.

The coughing fit passed, leaving her throat feeling raw. "Couldn't be better," she told him hoarsely, still refusing to look directly at him. She could feel his eyes on her.

"Looks to me like you're going to be stuck with us for a while, Red." Though Violet refused to look at him, she couldn't shut out his voice. There was just something about it; there had always been something about it. To Violet, his voice was rough and yet caressing at the same time. It was like being licked by a tomcat's tongue.

With a slight shudder, Violet forced the seductive image of a cat's tongue, licking, from her mind. She raised the drink to her lips again, and then decided that the last thing she could afford at the moment was to fog up her brain with alcohol. She plunked it down on the mantelpiece.

"I thought—" she seethed, finally making herself meet his eyes "—that you would at least have the common courtesy to allow me to talk to my mother alone about this."

He shook his head, looking infuriatingly amused. "I'm just not a courteous guy. Sorry, Red."

"You are not sorry in the least, and you know it." The words came out with a slight hiss because she had her teeth clenched.

He only chuckled, another of those rough, caressing sounds that seemed to heat her nerves and weaken her knees.

She could hear Glorianna and Lacy Jay laughing together in the kitchen. Slow was right about one thing, she realized. It was highly unlikely that she'd be able to get rid of Slow and the little girl before it was necessary for her to leave the condo herself.

And then she couldn't help thinking that getting her mother alone again wasn't likely to do her much good anyway. Glorianna hadn't budged an inch before Slow and his daughter arrived. There was little evidence to suggest that she would change her mind in the near future, no matter how much Violet pleaded, ranted and raved.

With an internal sigh, Violet conceded that her first option, convincing Glorianna to change her tune, had turned out a dead end. It was time to proceed with the only other approach she could think of: reasoning with Slow himself.

It was an option she dreaded exercising, she perceived in a sudden flash of disturbing insight. And, in all honesty, she'd been frantically running from actually having to talk to him since the moment he'd appeared on her front porch. But running, as was often the case, had gotten her nowhere. It was time to stand and deal with Slow face-to-face.

Violet looked across the room and met Slow's eyes. He gazed back at her, leaning on an elbow, an index finger against his lips. His eyebrows lifted, as if he read in her expression that she was about to change tactics in this cat-and-mouse game they'd been playing.

"I can hear that mind of yours ticking away," Slow said when long, tense seconds had passed with only silence between them.

"We have to talk. Alone," she said flatly.

Slow thought about that, running his teeth over his knuckle very lightly, making her think of tomcats and their stroking tongues all over again. "After all these years, now you're willing to talk?" He made a low sound in his throat, a sound both bitter and amused.

"Not about the past," she snapped too quickly. "That's over. That's nothing to either of us now."

He nodded, one long, slow raising and lowering of his head. "Okay. The past is nothing. And you want to talk about right now."

"It's a reasonable request, I think."

"Sure. Reasonable." He kept stroking his knuckle with his white, even teeth and staring at her.

And, unbidden at this utterly inappropriate moment, she experienced a memory so vivid it might have been happening right then.

It was a memory of the two of them on a certain summer night when she was seventeen, sitting at the dining room table at the Windemere house. The next night, though neither of them knew it then, he would be caught joyriding in Darrell's father's Corvette and given the choice of jail or the army. But this was the night before he finally went too far and was virtually run out of town. This was the night that he kissed her for the first time.

She'd been drilling him on his Latin verbs. *His* father had asked *her* father if she would help him with his Latin, though it was clear to Violet, as she sat there reeling off verb tenses while Slow stared into space, that Slow had little or no interest in conjugating verbs.

He'd been wearing black, just as he was now, and he'd been slumped down in the straight chair, his legs sprawled out in front of him, alternately looking at the ceiling and the floor. Violet had sat, straight as a broom handle, in her plain blouse and skirt, trying not to think about the forbidden feelings he roused in her—feelings no one else knew about, which had been bothering her since she was at least fifteen.

For almost an hour she'd tried to get him to work on the task at hand, but he had responded with only grunts and an occasional grumbled, "Whatever, sure, that's cool..."

Finally she'd slammed the book shut and glared at him.

"Why in the world are you here?"

Slow's head came up at that and he looked directly at her. "Who the hell knows? One last effort to please the old man, I guess."

She snapped back. "Effort? What effort? You're not making any effort."

He shrugged. "'Cause it ain't gonna work. I don't need Latin to do what I want to do." He stood up then and loomed above her, looking down. "Sorry about wasting your time, Red."

She realized he was about to go, and something inside her ached at the thought. The whole thing was terribly confusing, because, for as long as she could remember, she'd despised Winslow Larkin.

When she was a little girl, he was forever tearing her dress or pulling her hair. As she grew to puberty, she'd learned to just stay away from him. But then, the past few years, every time she saw him, she had these aching, longing feelings that made no sense at all.

She was thinking about that, about those feelings. And she'd looked up at him to tell him something sharp and final, something like, "Fine, goodbye, see you around." But those feelings must have been there, softening her eyes.

He had looked down at her, his own eyes changing, and she'd known that *he* knew.

He blinked, and then he smiled, a *real* smile, not the smirky ones he usually gave her. He said, kind of quiet and hesitant, "You want to walk out with me?"

If he was hesitant, she was not. She stood and set the Latin book on the table.

"Yes," she said, and followed him out...

"All right, Red." The past melted into the present. The grown-up Slow Larkin was responding to her request. "We'll talk."

Violet heard her mother's lusty laughter approaching from the kitchen; Glorianna and Lacy Jay were coming back.

"Good," Violet murmured, feeling dazed. He was sitting across from her, fifteen years older and up to no good. Yet she kept remembering his voice, way back then, so sweet and gentle, asking her to come outside...

"I'm calling Arthur right now, Slow," Glorianna proclaimed as she swept back into the room. "We're taking you and Lacy Jay to the county fair tonight. We'll see every exhibit, and ride every ride, and stuff ourselves with cotton candy and pink popcorn until we're fat enough to burst.''

Slow left off pinning Violet with his stare and smiled at Glorianna. It was a simple, friendly smile. For a moment Violet felt cheated. The smiles Slow turned *her* way were cruel, ironic, sensual and cold by turns, but never friendly. But then, she reproached herself, she didn't want his friendship. She wanted him to leave her alone and let her get on with her life.

''How about tomorrow night?'' he suggested. ''Lacy Jay needs a good night's rest after the long ride today.''

''Aw, Dad...'' Lacy Jay whined, in the voice of all disappointed children everywhere.

But Glorianna put an arm around her slender shoulders and gave her a squeeze. ''Your father's right. I didn't think. Tomorrow will be here before you know it.''

''I guess.'' Lacy Jay looked doubtful about tomorrow ever coming, but resigned to her fate of a good night's sleep.

Slow rose from the chair. ''Lacy, stay here with Glory for a while, okay?''

''Why?'' The question held none of the sulky challenge one might have expected from some children. It was clear that the girl was simply curious.

''I need to talk to Violet for a few minutes.''

''About whether she's going to kick us out or not?''

Slow and Glorianna exchanged a look. ''More or less,'' Slow answered.

Violet wished again that getting rid of Slow didn't add up to a tacit rejection of his child in the bargain.

But she didn't know what she could say or do that would soften the truth. After all, she *did* want to get rid of Slow, and Lacy Jay went with him.

"We won't be long," she murmured inanely and reached over the back of the couch to take her shoulder bag from the table.

"Take your time, my love," Glorianna advised with an indulgent smile as Violet moved into the hall.

Violet reached for the front doorknob, only to have Slow beat her to it.

"Allow me," he said in a mockery of courtliness. Without a word she stepped back for him to open the door. Then she went out into the August sunlight with Slow Larkin close behind.

"Don't worry about Lacy Jay," Slow said a few minutes later when they were strolling the tree-shaded paths that meandered between the buildings. "She's not the kind to hold a grudge."

Violet glanced at him from the corner of her eye, surprised at the way he seemed to have picked up her concern for his daughter's feelings without her ever having said what she felt in words. She almost opened her mouth to tell him thank-you, for understanding how she felt, for easing her mind.

But she decided that she couldn't afford to be thanking him right then; she was supposed to be getting rid of him. They came to a bridge that spanned the small man-made stream flowing around the property. They paused, in silent accord, in the middle of the bridge and leaned on the railing to look down at the shallow water below.

The stream wasn't swift, so Violet could see their reflections looking back at them. Herself and Slow Larkin, standing side by side, after all these years....

Another of those strange, vertiginous shivers slid over her skin. Since he'd knocked on her door, it had been like this. She'd be doing fine, and then it would strike her anew: Slow Larkin had returned—and the world had turned upside down.

She didn't realize she'd closed her eyes in a vain effort to control her emotional light-headedness until Slow grabbed her hand.

"Come on," he instructed. She wanted to jerk away, but she felt numb all over—except for her hand. That felt warm and alive because he was holding it. She dragged her feet but didn't really protest as he pulled her along behind him. At a wooden bench beneath a willow tree a few feet from the bridge, he stopped. "Sit down here."

Violet's knees obligingly gave way. Slow sat down beside her. She looked dazedly down at their clasped hands and knew she had to get hold of herself.

She reclaimed her hand and put it in her lap.

"Come on, Red," Slow said, his voice coaxing, after they had been sitting for a few minutes listening to a squawky argument between two blackbirds on a wire overhead. "It's just not that bad."

She turned on him. "It's impossible. You can't just...pop up after eleven years and move into my house!"

He gave her one of his best bad-boy smiles. "Maybe I can't—but I am."

"But *why?*"

"Why not?"

"A thousand reasons. Because I'm going to marry Darrell, to name just one."

He looked at her for a moment, his expression bland. Then he drawled, "Congratulations. But I don't see a ring."

"I haven't formally said yes yet."

"Ah. You're saying yes tonight?"

"Not that it's any of your business but, yes, I am."

"Well." He looked up at the bickering blackbirds for a minute and then back at her. "I hope you'll be happy." His face remained unreadable; his tone was as polite as she'd ever heard it. She didn't believe him for one second.

"If you want me to be happy," she replied tightly, "then find somewhere else to stay."

He stretched those long, strong legs out in front of him and crossed his booted feet at the ankles. "Can't do that, Red."

"But *why?*" she demanded again. Her voice held a desperate edge, and she didn't even try to mask it. At this point, she would do just about anything to get through to him. "You have to realize how your staying in my house will only cause trouble—"

"I like making trouble," he said lazily. "Always did and always will."

"Oh, stop it," she snapped. "That's a bald-faced lie and you know it. Your mother died when you were born, and you and your father never came to any kind of understanding. You made trouble because you felt unacknowledged and discouraged as a person. But since then, from what my mother's told me and from what I can see with my own eyes when I look at Lacy Jay, you've figured out exactly who you are and you're leading a productive, effective life. You don't need to make trouble anymore to get attention, Slow, so my bet is that you don't *bother* to make a lot of trouble as a general rule.''

He chuckled. ''You're no idiot, Red. I'll give you that much.''

''The question is, why do you want to make trouble for me—given that you're a grown man with a daughter to raise and, presumably, plenty to do without taking a few weeks off to drive an old girlfriend out of her mind. It just doesn't make sense. Why, after all these years and all the bad blood between the two of us, would you have any desire to share the same roof with me anyway?''

Slow gave her a level stare, one free, for once, of cynicism. ''That's a damn good question, Red.''

''So answer it.'' Violet became aware of a rising feeling of anticipation in her stomach. Maybe—just maybe—they were finally going to get beyond this pointless game of hide-and-seek they'd been playing.

But he said nothing. As the silence stretched out, Violet fervently wished for just a peek at what was going on behind his hooded eyes.

Chapter Three

Slow Larkin stared at the little red-haired witch sitting beside him and had no idea what to say to her. How could he answer her question, when he himself didn't fully understand what was driving him?

He'd called Glory last week and learned that Violet was going to tie the knot with Darrell Carruthers—and suddenly it had seemed a matter of life and death to get up to Nevada City and start a new life for himself and Lacy Jay. He'd told Glory his plans, she'd offered the Windemere house as a place to stay and he'd accepted without missing a beat.

He'd put himself on cruise control after that—acting and not thinking, just doing what he felt compelled to do.

He'd spent five days tying up loose ends at Classic Cars, Incorporated, and closing up the house in North Hollywood. Now, today—here he was. Planning to start all over again in the hometown to which he'd always sworn he would *never* return.

He had this half-baked plan to open a shop here, to do restorations on a small scale, performing most of the work himself and then jobbing out whatever he wasn't equipped to handle. It was not a very bright idea, if he looked at it critically.

He'd already created a company that was revolutionizing the car restoration business. At Classic Cars, Incorporated, he had more than fifty employees. And they did it all, from the frame up, on-site and in a reasonable time frame. To return to doing everything himself, with maybe a hydraulic lift as his most sophisticated piece of equipment, would be like voluntarily going back to the Dark Ages. Totally wacko.

But strangely enough, every moment he was here, every moment he looked through Red's glasses and into those green eyes, he was more sure that he wasn't leaving until—

Until what? Hell, he didn't really know.

Maybe, he thought wryly, the real answer to Red's question was that he'd finally gone over the deep end for good. Maybe it had happened back there on her porch, in that moment when she tried to help Lacy Jay with the bags and he'd reached out a hand to stop her—and he'd felt as if someone had smacked him in the chest with a tire iron.

Or maybe it had been later, up in her old man's big bedroom with the velvet curtains and the furniture that some prehistoric Windemere must have had shipped in on the *Mayflower*. He'd stretched out on the bed and put his hands behind his head—and looked at Red's legs.

And he'd remembered, in detail, what she could be like once he got her going. It got him hot, plain and simple. Just like it always had.

Just like the first time he'd kissed her, when she was seventeen and supposed to be drilling him in Latin. Then, all those years ago, he'd stood and said he was leaving, and she'd looked up suddenly—and behind the lenses of her ugly glasses he'd seen it all.

Little Miss Perfect had the hots for him—for bad Slow Larkin, though she'd always pretended he wasn't good enough to wipe the soles of her penny loafers. She had the hots for him. And, absurdly, the sudden realization had made *him* hot. Hot, and hopeful, and eager as hell. Fifteen years later it was still the same. Just thinking about that night, even now, made his jeans too tight.

He'd asked her, scared to death she might say no, to come out with him. And she'd said yes so sweet and simply, then followed him out. They had gone to the back porch swing and they'd sat, not even swinging, for a few minutes, both of them hardly daring to move.

But at last he'd kissed her. And things had gotten very hot very fast.

Red was like that once she finally let go, a female fire out of control. He'd been eighteen then, and plenty willing to give her just what she was panting for. He'd made short work of getting her blouse unbuttoned, her bra out of the way and one of those beautiful white breasts of hers cradled in his hand.

At that moment, her father, who was every bit as much of a pompous ass as his own old man, had discovered them. To Slow's list of transgressions was added the attempted ravishment of the proper Miss Windemere.

Then the next night there had been the little problem with the Carrutherses' Corvette. They'd given him a choice after that stunt: the army or jail. He'd chosen Uncle Sam. There was nothing for him in Nevada City anyway. He'd never planned to come back.

But four years later his father had lain dying of cancer. Slow had come back, to see the old tyrant one final time and, after that, to bury him. The proper Miss Windemere had been home from college between semesters and she'd sought Slow out, to express her condolences. They'd been all over each other in five minutes flat.

She had sworn then that she'd follow him anywhere. But when her old man had found them together, she'd changed her tune. She'd chosen her safe, well-planned future over taking a chance on the man she claimed to love.

It still twisted his gut, every time he remembered how he'd begged her to come with him. She had cried and sworn how sorry she was. But she'd still sent him away.

"Slow, please. We really do need to get it all out in the open," she said now, from beside him. She sounded less hostile than she had been. Maybe she sensed that he was at least considering getting down to some truth with her.

But now he was angry at her again. He'd talked himself all the way around from a reluctant urge to get honest with her to the need to keep baiting her.

He wanted revenge, he supposed, for the way she'd hurt him once. Fresh in his mind again was the memory of how he'd held out his heart to her—and she'd pitched it right back in his face.

"Slow, you do see, don't you—I mean, now that you've thought about it—how absurd this whole thing really is?"

She was looking at him. Her mouth, which was not wide or full but mobile and shaped to be kissed, quivered just the tiniest fraction at one corner.

The quiver did something to him; it sent a straight bolt of lust right down into his vitals. The quiver proved, if he'd had any doubt, that he still got to her. She was a fully mature woman now, and a practicing attorney. In ninety-nine percent of all situations, he was damn sure she would have no problem controlling the muscles of her face. But she'd been looking alternately dreamy and faint, furious and frightened, since the moment she'd opened her front door to him.

"You know, you're right," he told her and laid his hand along the back of the bench behind her. "I've been totally out of line. My staying with you would only stir up a lot of old resentments. It's just not a good idea."

The little quiver in her lip was swallowed by her relieved smile. Behind the rims of her glasses, her eyes shone with frank gratitude. She had heard just what she'd wanted to hear and assumed he'd be leaving her house.

Then she felt the brush of his arm against her back. She gave a small cough and sat forward a fraction. She said, her voice turned cordial since she assumed she could afford to be polite now, "I *can* understand your desire, as a single parent, to provide a nurturing environment for your daughter, though. And Nevada City is a wonderful place to raise a child."

Slow glanced away. He personally felt that it didn't much matter where a kid was raised, as long as they got fed right and received the love and attention they needed. But there was no way he would admit that now, since he was presumably here to give Lacy Jay a white-picket-fence, storybook kind of childhood.

"But I wonder," Violet went on, "if uprooting Lacy Jay from the only home she's ever known so soon after she's lost her mother is really the best way to go."

Slow's shoulders tensed. Her observation had hit home.

His wife, Loni, a motion-picture stuntwoman, had died in a filming accident a little more than a year ago. Lacy had been devastated at first. But after a few months, she'd begun laughing and smiling easily once more. Her performance in school had remained exceptional. Moreover, there had been *no* signs that the rather tough neighborhood they lived in was having an adverse effect on her.

In his heart, Slow agreed with what Violet had just said; dragging Lacy to a new place now might not be the best thing for her.

To cover his defensiveness, Slow inquired sarcastically, "Ever notice that people without kids always seem to be experts on how to raise them?"

Violet looked away, and he saw that he'd hurt her. "Of course, you're right," she said, her voice reserved and polite. "She seems like a very well-adjusted child, so whatever you're doing must be working just fine."

Slow's defensiveness faded. Now he felt like a jerk. He already knew how Violet felt about children. She wanted them. That was evidenced in her sincere interest in Lacy Jay—not to mention some of the things she'd told him way back when.

This whole thing, he realized, was damn confusing for him, too. He wanted to somehow settle the old score with her, but at the same time he hated to see her eyes cloud over with hurt. He glanced away from her just as she was looking away from him, thinking of the way she'd been on the bridge a few minutes ago, almost dizzy from the strain of having to deal with him again. He understood how she'd felt, because right now he felt exactly that way himself.

Maybe Red had it right. The past was over, finished, dead. And if he had any sense he'd climb in his Chevy and head back to North Hollywood where he and Lacy Jay probably belonged.

He was just about to turn to tell her that when she began fidgeting beside him. A sideways glance told him she was digging around in her purse. He turned to look at her directly just as she pulled out a checkbook. He watched, his eyes narrowing. She was writing out a check.

"What are you doing?" he asked quietly.

She stopped writing and rested her hand, still wrapped around her gold pen, on the checkbook. She looked at him, a patient yet take-charge sort of look. "Mother's condo is a little small for three people, so I want to pay for your hotel while you and Lacy Jay look for a suitable place of your own."

He felt the heat of anger once again. A slow, relentless sort of burn. Some things never changed. There were people who thought all they needed to do to get things their way was to write out a check—or hold one back. His old man had been that way.

In a tone that was meant to appease, Violet said, "Slow, please. Don't be offended. This is not an insult to your manhood or anything. I know very well that you have plenty of money of your own now. It's only fair, that's all. It's because of me that you now have no place to stay, so I want to see that you're made comfortable elsewhere."

He spoke again, still quietly. "That's real thoughtful of you, Red."

She tried a smile but it wavered. Clearly she sensed that her offer of money wasn't going down quite right. "Please don't be offended," she said again.

He looked at her, at her hair that shone vivid as flame in the sunlight and her shaky smile and the smattering of freckles across her slim nose. She wasn't beautiful, but somehow she seemed far more alluring than any woman he had ever known.

Slow was no Casanova, but he'd been around a little—during his stint in the service, especially. And there had never been a woman who could do for him what Violet had done—with a kiss when he was eighteen and with her whole luminous, slender body four years after that.

Maybe he'd driven more than four hundred miles just to find out if he still felt that old urge when he looked at her—the urge to get her into the nearest porch swing and start to work on the buttons of her blouse.

Well, he guessed he'd found out all right. The old urge was still there, heating his blood and tightening his jeans.

Unfortunately, tonight she was going to tell another man she'd marry him. And not just any *other* man, but Darrell Carruthers, with whom Slow also had a few unsettled scores.

He wondered, looking at her now, just how much she knew about dear old Straight-Arrow Darrell. Did she know how it had really gone down the night they ran Slow out of town for joyriding in Darrell's father's '63 Stingray split-window coupe? Or about the check Darrell had tried to write him four years after that? The amount had been five thousand dollars, to leave Nevada City—and Violet—and never come back.

Beside him on the little bench, Violet cleared her throat and tried again, "Slow?"

"What?"

"You do understand, then, about the check?"

He chuckled. "I understand completely."

She stared at him, looking kind of hypnotized for a moment more, and then bent her head to sign her name.

He laid his hand over hers. She froze, and then her head shot up. "Slow?" There was a little catch in her voice, a little husky, hungry catch. Slow savored that catch, more proof that she still wanted the same thing she'd always wanted from him—which, he was thinking, he just might decide to give her before this was through.

"I just can't take your money," he said rather tenderly.

Violet swallowed. "Wh-why not?"

His lips curled upward in a lazy, triumphant smirk. "Because I'm not leaving your house."

Slowly, like someone who feared spooking a dangerous animal, she pulled her hand away. Then she said, in a low, very controlled tone, "You bastard. You purposely let me think you would move out."

He shrugged. "I gave it some thought. And I decided it won't kill you to give an old friend a place to stay for a while."

"We are not friends."

"Whatever. It doesn't matter. I'm staying put."

"I dislike you intensely at this moment."

"That's supposed to be news?"

"I want you out of my house."

"I gathered."

"I will pay for your accommodations."

"You said that."

"Then go. Just say you'll go."

"The answer is no."

She stared at him, stricken. And then she gave up and tried pleading with him. "Please, Slow. *Please...* Find somewhere else to stay."

Slow looked at her face and read the pain and confusion written there. He knew his very presence challenged all that she was. A part of him ached for her, for her bewilderment at the way the old fires she'd thought long dead were suddenly flaring again, promising that, given half an opportunity, they'd once more rage out of control.

But then he remembered his own pain eleven years before, how he'd cried like a baby and begged her not to walk out the door. She'd gone anyway.

Maybe it was about time she had a taste of her own medicine.

"Tell you what, Red," he said, as if he were actually making some kind of concession. "I'll do my best to stay out of your hair, how's that?"

"What do you mean?"

"Lacy Jay and I will stay upstairs and leave the downstairs to you."

"I'm supposed to be grateful for that?"

He shrugged. "Grateful or not, it's the best I can do."

"But even if you use the back stairs—" she groaned "—we'll still have to share the *kitchen.*"

Slow had to restrain a laugh. She made sharing the kitchen sound as intimate as sharing a bed. But then maybe it was. For the two of them.

Chapter Four

"My God, Violet, how in the world can you have let this occur?" Darrell demanded.

They were sitting in a secluded corner of the Holbrooke Restaurant, in Grass Valley's legendary hotel of the same name. The walls around them were warm, aged brick, the carpet a lush forest green. Linen so white it gleamed covered their table, and the champagne that Darrell had curtly ordered waited in a bucket nearby.

But Darrell wasn't thinking about the ambience. He was fuming, just as he had been doing since the moment he'd stepped into Violet's living room and discovered Slow Larkin and Lacy Jay sprawled on the rug, sharing a big bowl of popcorn and watching a movie on the VCR.

Darrell tugged angrily at his tie, loosening it a little. "And why in heaven's name didn't you *warn* me?"

he accused. "Can you possibly imagine how I felt, arriving to pick you up, completely unaware, and finding that troublemaking bum—"

"He's not a bum," Violet interjected without even stopping to consider how jumping to Slow's defense might sound. "Not really. In actuality, he's done quite well for himself." Darrell was glaring at her. She finished sheepishly, "He just . . . looks like a bum."

"Are you defending him?" Darrell asked, sounding the way she imagined he might sound if she'd told him that Adolf Hitler had really been a warm-hearted guy.

"No, of course not." Violet made her voice brisk. "I'm just stating the facts. He owns a very successful car restoration business in Southern California. I'll lay you odds he's richer than you and me put together—"

Darrell didn't want to hear about how rich Slow Larkin was. He cut her off. "You've completely changed the subject on me. I asked you why you didn't at least warn me he was there."

"I didn't have time, Darrell."

"What do you mean? Surely a phone call would have been possible."

Violet pushed away the delicious stuffed pork chop that she'd barely touched. The waiter immediately removed the plate; Violet gave him a distracted smile.

"Are you going to answer me or not, Violet?"

Violet sipped her champagne, which had started to go flat. "When I got back to the house after trying to reason with my mother, I had twenty minutes to get ready before you arrived. There wasn't time, Darrell." She spoke very evenly, staring straight into his eyes.

Darrell drank from his own champagne glass. When he set it down, it clinked against his butter knife. He was the first to break eye contact, and she knew he was realizing that he had carried things a little too far. "I apologize," he said evenly after a moment. "I'm upset by this. I'm behaving like an imbecile."

She forced a smile. "It's all right. It's...difficult for both of us."

He reached across and took her hand. "Darling, there's only one thing to do in this situation. You'll come and stay with me. At least until he leaves."

Violet studied Darrell's face, from his serious gray eyes to his smooth but slightly stubborn chin. His suggestion was a logical one; it would neatly solve the problem that neither of them quite wanted to put into words.

And, of course, Darrell had several bedrooms in his beautiful new house on Ridge Road. If she still felt she wasn't ready for the big step of physical intimacy with him yet, he would not argue if she chose a room alone.

But then, eclipsing the nice, handsome face across from her, she saw taunting deep blue eyes and a lazy, wicked smile. Without even thinking about it, she jerked her hand free of Darrell's grip.

"No," she said. "Slow Larkin is not putting me out of my own home."

Darrell's expression clouded again, but his voice remained coaxing. "Darling, you must see reason about this—"

Violet cut him off. "I said no, Darrell. Thank you for the offer, but no."

"It's totally inappropriate for you to stay under the same roof with him."

Violet began to feel stifled, and she fought the feeling by demanding rather belligerently, "What do you mean, inappropriate?"

"Violet." Now he was sounding reproachful, as if she were a not-very-bright child. "Let's not resurrect all the old unpleasantness, all right?"

The feeling that she was being smothered increased. Perhaps it was his condescending tone. So aloof, so superior, so overbearingly self-righteous. So much like—

Violet caught her thoughts up short, but not in time. In the back of her mind that voice of defiance whispered, *my father,* even as she tried to shut it out.

Hardly aware that Darrell was speaking again, she tried to wash away the guilty taste in her mouth with another sip of champagne. It seemed wrong to think such critical thoughts about a dead man who couldn't defend himself. Besides, Clovis Windemere had been a good man, a man who'd always done the right thing.

But then she remembered something her mother had said shortly after Clovis died, when Violet had been trying to understand the mystery of her parents' relationship.

"We loved each other," Glorianna had explained. "We *adored* each other. We could never, ever, forget each other! Unfortunately, though, we also could never *agree* on anything. He thought I was a fallen woman whom it was his destiny to save, and I thought he was a prig—an incredibly sexy old prig, but a prig, nonetheless. You see, my love, your father was always sure he knew what was right—and he took it upon himself to force the rest of us to live by his rules. He married me because I excited him, and then immediately set out to try and change me—which he couldn't do, and for which I eventually left him. But then, as I said, I still loved him. As he still loved me. That's why neither of us ever quite got around to divorcing, and why I returned to him when he became so ill..."

"Violet, are you listening to me?" Darrell asked from across the table.

"Yes. Sorry. I was just...thinking is all." Violet ordered her mind to stick to the subject at hand. The waiter came by with the dessert tray. Violet waved it away, but nodded yes to coffee.

"What I've been trying to say is, if you won't come and stay with me, then there's only one thing left to do."

"There is?"

"Absolutely."

"What is it?" Violet looked at him hopefully over the rim of the coffee cup she was raising to her lips. When it came to Slow Larkin's residence in her home, she herself was out of ideas. If Darrell had thought of something that hadn't occurred to her, she'd be grateful.

Darrell announced nobly, "I will have to have a talk with him."

With a sharp clink, Violet set her cup back in its saucer. She could hardly believe what she was hearing. One thing she'd always appreciated about Darrell was the way he treated her as an equal. But she was seeing another side of him tonight, one she didn't like at all.

"Darrell Carruthers, you will do nothing of the kind."

Darrell stared at her for a brief moment, probably somewhat stunned at the steel in her tone. Then he

blustered on, "Violet, if you can't handle the problem yourself—"

Violet raised her hand, a small controlled gesture.
"It is *my* problem. Not yours."

"But if I talked to him, man-to-man—"

"Darrell, I am a thirty-two-year-old woman with a
law degree and a good head on my shoulders. And I
refuse to be treated like a bone between two dogs."
She paused for a moment to let what she'd said sink
in. When she spoke again, her tone was softer but no
less determined. "Please don't get into it with him,
Darrell. I mean it. It's my problem and I'll handle it."

Darrell listened, his face impassive, while she spoke.
When she was finished, he didn't reply right away.
Then his eyes shifted away, and she had a fleeting impression of furtiveness, which was something she
never would have used to describe Darrell before.

"Of course," he said finally. "If you insist."

"I do." She forced herself to touch his arm, though
the gesture felt all wrong. She was trying to commu-
nicate that she appreciated his acceptance of her position.

She pulled her hand back right away, thinking un-
comfortably how strange it all was. Slow Larkin
showed up in town and she immediately started imag-
ining things about Darrell that had never even crossed
her mind in the past. She suddenly saw her father's
imperiousness in him, and thought he was behaving
furtively when all he'd done was glance away.

I must be overtired, she thought. My reactions are
just all out of whack from everything that's happened today. I've known Darrell all my life and I work
with him every day. He's a good, kind man who
couldn't be furtive if he tried.

She looked at him and smiled. "Darrell, this was a lovely dinner. I'm just sorry I couldn't appreciate it more. But it's been an awful day, and I think it would be best if we just—-tried this another time."

His expression was suddenly a portrait of solicitousness. "I've upset you. I'm sorry."

"No, no. It's not really you. It's...everything. I really would just like to go home."

"But, darling. We can't call it a night quite yet."

"Darrell, I just think it would be better—"

"Let's just put aside all this unpleasantness, why don't we? This...thing with Slow Larkin has been blown way out of proportion. If he insists on invading your house and Glorianna aids and abets him, well, that's just how it is. For now. We'll see how things develop once we've had a little time to consider other...alternatives."

"Darrell, I mean it. I will handle Slow."

"Certainly, whatever you say."

"Thank you. And now I'd like to go home, please."

"But you can't go, not yet." Now his tone reproached her again. "Have you forgotten...your promise?"

There it was, Violet thought grimly. The subject she'd been guiltily dreading all night. "No, Darrell, I haven't forgotten."

"You asked me to give you a week to think it over. And I have been more than patient, wouldn't you say?" His rather small mouth formed a tight little smile. "I haven't even *mentioned* it all week. True to my word, as always."

"I know. You've been thoughtful and considerate. And I do appreciate that."

"Thank you. And now..." He gazed at her, waiting, his gray eyes full of tender expectation.

She looked back at him and remembered that she'd already made her decision. She'd thought it all out and knew that a life with him was exactly what she wanted.

But somehow she just couldn't bring herself to say it. Instead she told him gently, "Everything's just been too crazy today, Darrell. We need to talk about it some other time."

For a split second his whole pleasant face looked hard as stone. Then he seemed to force his expression to relax. "When, exactly, will you be willing to talk about it?"

Violet opened her mouth to give another evasive answer, and then held it back because it came to her that an evasive answer would be utterly unfair to Darrell.

She'd told him *no* for years. During that time it had been *his* responsibility if he insisted on asking again and again.

But since her father had died, and she'd started to feel as if the important things in life might be passing her by, she'd begun to encourage Darrell. She'd started seeking him out more often at the office, to go over a fine point of law or to ask his advice on an approach to a case.

They'd begun going to lunch every few days. And then dating on weekends.

And then, last Saturday, when he'd popped the question, she'd been frankly receptive. She'd made it sound like the week she needed to think it over was no more than a formality.

Which was exactly what it was. Then.

But now she had to admit, after what had happened today, that maybe marrying Darrell wasn't the right choice for her. How could she say yes to Darrell when simply laying her hand on Slow Larkin's arm had turned her knees to spaghetti and sent her heart rocketing into her throat? It just wasn't right.

She said, "Darrell, I—"

But Darrell, who seemed to sense she might be about to say the opposite of what he wanted to hear, didn't let her go on. "Wait. You're right. I'm being an insensitive clod. It's been a horrendous day for you, and you're in absolutely no condition to be pressured into saying you'll marry me tonight. A better time will come. We'll just let it go for now." He reached for her hand again, and she, feeling once more as if to even let him touch her was wrong, had to force herself not to pull away.

At the same moment, a few miles away in the big house on East Broad Street, Slow Larkin stood at the window in the living room and ordered himself not to sneak another peek through the lace curtains that blocked his view of the street.

He wandered through the front hall into the formal, old-fashioned parlor, where the brocade couches looked too fancy to sit on and the heavily scrolled side tables had fringed shawls on top of them. The big clock on the mantel that looked as if it had been carved out of a large chunk of somebody's tombstone said nine-fifteen.

He'd carried Lacy Jay, dead to the world, upstairs just half an hour ago. And he'd been roaming from room to room ever since.

What's she doing now? he wondered, though he'd told himself about a million times that he didn't give a damn what was going on between Violet and Darrell Carruthers tonight.

Has she told him yes yet? Is he kissing her?

It's none of my damn business. Why should I care?

But he did care. He cared way too much.

Slow dropped to the bench of the upright piano that stood against the wall adjoining the window that looked out on the front yard. He leaned backward and braced his elbows on the fallboard, sticking his legs out into the room. He studied his boots as if there were something new about them.

What the hell am I doing here? What the hell am I after?

Is it revenge?

His head shot up as he thought of the word. Blindly he stared at a pair of Mathis etchings on the far wall while he thought about that.

Revenge. Maybe.

It could be called that.

What he wanted was Violet. At least one more time. He wanted her to come to him willingly, and offer herself, and he wanted to hold her off for a while, make sure she was really gone—hungry and needy— before he gave her what she was after. He wanted to be inside of her, sheathed in her, and to make her go wild.

He wanted to be damn sure that she remembered for the rest of her life exactly what she had once rejected.

It was a lousy, rotten thing to want. Slow knew that. But that didn't make him want it any less.

And the truth was that he and Violet were probably too different in temperament to ever make a perma- nent match anyway. They were like Clovis and Glory had been—opposites attracting, but not much good for each other when it came to the long haul.

Right now, though, Slow wasn't thinking a hell of a lot about the long haul. Right now he was thinking of the limits he was willing to impose on the prospect of the revenge he'd just let himself admit that he wanted.

He was thinking about Darrell Carruthers. He was thinking that he owed the other man exactly zero, for more reasons than one. He was thinking that Darrell *deserved* to find his fiancée in bed with bad Slow Larkin.

At that thought, Slow got up from the piano bench. He paced the stuffy, old-fashioned room. It was the word *fiancée* that was bothering him. A part of him hated messing things up for her, if Darrell Carruthers was really the man she wanted to spend her life with. Though it cut like a knife to think it, Violet and Carruthers were a good match for each other in a lot of ways. If she really wanted the other man, it was going to be doubly rotten and lousy of Slow to mess it up for her.

But then Slow thought about the little lustful quiver in her lip on the bench beneath the willow tree that afternoon. He thought about the husky, longing way she said his name. And he smiled to himself.

You're no idiot, Red, he had told her. And she wasn't.

He was willing to bet, now that he thought about it, that there'd be no ring when she showed up at the door tonight. She just wasn't going to be able to agree to marry Darrell Carruthers when the object of her forbidden lust—Slow himself—was waiting for her at home. He was willing to bet his revenge on it.

Slow chuckled to himself.

Fair enough, he decided. If she came home with a ring, he'd pack up Lacy Jay and be out of this old museum of a house in the morning. Otherwise...

Slow chuckled again. Anticipation curled in his belly. It was going to be *otherwise,* he was sure of it. She would walk back in the door tonight without a ring. And Slow Larkin would have his revenge.

Chapter Five

Violet gave Darrell a chaste peck on the lips at the front door. When he tried to get her to hold still for more, she slid nimbly out of the circle of his arms and slipped inside.

"Good night, Darrell." With what she hoped was an affectionate smile, she gently closed the door.

Then, feeling like a bouncing ball from which someone had suddenly released all the air, she put her forehead against the smooth wood that framed the glass at the top of the door and let out a long sigh.

"True love," said a low, taunting voice from the living room. "Can't it just wear you out?"

Violet's body went rigid. Here, at last, she had arrived home, the place that should have been a haven from all the trials of the day, only to find the cause of her problems waiting up for her.

She longed to beat the door with a clenched fist, or burst into frustrated tears, or lift her head heavenward and let out one long, agonized howl.

She did none of these things. Instead she doggedly pushed away from the door and forced her feet to carry her beneath the arch to the living room, where Slow sat sprawled in her father's favorite armchair. He had one of his car magazines open on his lap. Across the room, the TV was on with the sound down. The changing images cast a flickering light on his face and granted a devilish gleam to his eyes.

She strode directly to the television and flicked it off. "Do you recall," she asked with admirable civility, "that our agreement was for you to stay upstairs except for the use of the kitchen?"

He smiled then, in that maddening way of his, while his eyes looked her over. "I like that dress," he said, staring at her bare shoulders. "Black makes your skin look like vanilla ice cream—but where are your glasses?" He actually sounded a little sad, and though it was the last thing she wanted to do, she remembered what he'd told her earlier: he loved her glasses because of what she did when he got them off her.

"They're on the dresser in my room," she told him. "I do have contacts, you know—and who cares about that anyway?"

"I care, Red," he said, with so much playful reproach that she would have laughed if she hadn't been so mad at him.

"You're not getting me off the subject, no matter what you say. I asked you why you're down here now—and why you *were* down here this evening when Darrell came to pick me up."

"Would you believe there are no TVs up there?" He gave her a look that both mocked and teased.

"Fine." Violet dropped her evening bag on top of the television. Then she stalked to the couch, sat down and slipped off her high-heeled black shoes. "I'll buy you a TV tomorrow. Then you can stay where you said you'd stay."

She glanced up to see him staring at her stocking feet, and she experienced a sudden feeling of extreme vulnerability, as if there were something intimate and seductively erotic about her taking off her shoes in front of him. Without really realizing she was doing it, she curled her toes—and saw that *he* saw when his mouth curved up. His gaze slowly traveled up her legs as, under her little black dress, her heart started knocking in forbidden expectation.

His eyes, when they at last met hers, were full of laughter and challenge and enough heat to melt her had she really been made of vanilla ice cream. "Don't bother," he said softly.

She realized she'd forgotten what they were talking about. "What?"

"Don't bother to buy me a TV. I like this one. Because it's down here where you are."

How could it be happening? She didn't want it to happen. But it was. That mysterious attraction he had for her seemed to work like a drug on her senses, making it hard for her to think straight.

She decided that it was not only pointless but dangerous to go to battle with him over such a minor issue as his keeping to the upstairs. Let him go ahead and take over the house—but let him get out as soon as possible.

He kept watching her, his gaze traveling over the hollows and curves of her throat, her bare shoulders and the top swells of her breasts, and then drifting back to her face. She wished, absurdly, that it was October instead of August, then she'd have been wearing an evening wrap as protection from his lazy scrutiny.

"Exactly what kind of schedule are you on?" she managed to demand.

"Schedule for what?" He was doing that thing with his index finger again, nibbling the back of it very lightly with his teeth.

"Schedule for finding your own place," she said, hating the silly, breathy way she sounded.

He completely ignored her question and shot back one of his own. "So don't keep me in suspense, Red. Have you and Darrell set the date?"

"That is none of your affair. How long are you staying here?"

Still not answering her, he set his magazine on the table beside him, pausing in the middle of the action to toss her a knowing smirk. "Couldn't do it, huh?"

Violet longed to shout that he wasn't playing fair in not answering her question before barreling on with rude inquiries of his own. But she held back, because at that moment she became aware of her own tightly crossed legs and the self-protective way she'd wrapped her arms around herself. Her entire body screamed of defensiveness, while his, stretched out to take up the whole of her father's big chair, showed total self-assurance and effortless command.

She was getting nowhere by insisting he observe the rules of civilized interchange. She should know better than to expect Slow Larkin to play by the rules. He'd never played by the rules in his life. If she hoped to get anywhere with him, she was going to have to be flexible, at least.

Violet forced herself to uncross her legs and rest her hands on the couch on either side of her body. Then she said with studied, careful calm. "Couldn't do what?"

He stood, taking his sweet time about it. Once he was on his feet, he stretched, and she found herself thinking that his body possessed a deep grace. That grace was partly because of the slow, sinuous way of moving he had—but it also seemed a quality of his flesh, inborn, like the color of his eyes or the tempting shape of his mouth, which was firm on the top and sightly fuller below.

"Couldn't quite get that word out," he said.

"What word?" Her voice sounded far away, dreamy. She was trying to keep the thread of this ridiculous excuse for a discussion, and all the while her mind kept wandering off to ponder things like the way Slow moved, or the shape of his lips.

"The *y* word. As in yes." He took a step toward her, only one step. Violet felt that step all the way down to her toes, which she once more nervously curled against the carpet. "Take my advice," he went on, and took another step.

Violet stared at him, thinking now about the sudden quick flickers of heat that had begun tickling all her nerve endings, making her skin prickle with taboo excitement. "Wh-what advice?"

He took another step, and another, and the sound of her heart was a throbbing in her ears, a heavy, building beat of mingled alarm and anticipation. Virtually hypnotized by his grace and the turncoat desires of her own body, she watched him approach, raising her head once he loomed above her.

He reached down. And his hand whispered along the soft skin of her throat.

Oh Lord, how could she have forgotten the things Slow's hands could do? How could she have forgotten the gentle, rousing care with which his fingers had once drifted lazily over every inch of her naked body, coaxing her ever nearer to the quivering brink of a shattering satisfaction?

Now the skin of his palm against her throat felt slightly rough, a wonderful roughness that made her long to stroke herself against it. Once, there had been faint dark stains around his nails and finger joints that he couldn't quite scrub away, testimony to his obsession for making old cars like new again.

Were those stains still there? She hadn't even noticed, had she? She'd been so busy trying *not* to notice. Not to let herself remember any of the details, the thousand little, separate things and attributes that made up Slow Larkin, the man, her one-time, week-long lover all those years ago.

He cupped her chin, his touch so warm it seemed to burn. "Tell him no," he said.

She looked up at him, unable to say a single word, only biting her lip a little to restrain herself from begging him to give her his mouth to taste and touch and know again.

"Tell him no," Slow instructed once more. "He'll never be able to satisfy you anyway." Violet blinked, the sensual haze that had settled over her thinning a bit as she registered exactly what he was saying. He continued, "You haven't slept with him yet, have you?"

That did it. She found, blessedly, that she was perfectly capable of moving now. In a quick, angry maneuver, she knocked his hand away and slid to the side, leaping from the couch as soon as she was beyond the formidable barrier his body created.

She backed toward her father's easy chair in the center of the room, trying to regain her shattered composure and formulate a scathing response at the same time.

He turned, chuckling now. "Or if you *have* gone to bed with him, it wasn't any good. That was obvious when he put his arm around your shoulders just before you left tonight. You . . . tolerated his touch. And that's all. Body language. It tells so much."

"You . . . you are despicable."

He faked a hurt look. "Aw, come on, Red. You can do better than that. Call me a rat-bastard. Call me something with a little *punch.*"

"Why are you doing this to me?" she asked, her voice hollow.

"Doing what?"

"You know what," she accused, glancing away. Now she was beginning to feel ashamed. She had come within a hairbreadth, there on the couch, of begging him for a kiss—and she had a horrible premonition that, given one kiss, she would never have been willing to let it end there. She forced herself to look back at him as she heard him drop to the place she'd vacated on the far end of the couch.

He was quiet, watching her, and she almost dared to hope, as she had that afternoon, that he was about to say something truthful for once. His cynical expression seemed to have softened. But perhaps that was just a trick of the light, which was coming from the lamp by her father's chair behind her and didn't really reach to where he sat.

The seconds ticked by, though, and she decided that if he *was* thinking honest thoughts, he wasn't going to share them. He said nothing.

"You are tormenting me, and you know it," she said into the lengthening silence. "Did you come back to town to... get even, is that it? Is that what's going on?"

"Get even for what, Red?"

"You know what. For... the past. For what happened eleven years ago, when I didn't go with you even though I said I would."

"Why? Is that something you feel guilty about?" If there had been any softness in his expression it was gone now. His voice sounded hard as the midnight-black shine on that artifact of the fifties that sat waiting on the curb out front.

"It's over, Slow," she said ardently. "What happened happened. We can't go back and undo it, surely you can see that."

"You didn't answer my question."

Violet sighed and rubbed her eyes, which felt grainy beneath her contact lenses. A headache, born of stress, had begun pressing at her temples.

A part of her longed to simply turn and leave the room. But the stubborn fighter deep within her couldn't quite give up yet. She had to try just once more to get through to him.

"The answer is yes," she said flatly. "I feel a little guilty about my behavior back then. I promised I'd go with you and I broke my promise. But I know it was the right decision. It takes more than... what we had to make a lasting relationship."

He picked up her hesitation and refused to let it pass. "What do you mean, *what we had?*"

"You know what I mean."

"Fine. So say it."

"Slow—"

"Say it."

"I..."

"Come on, Red. Get it out. You can do it." The words were a blatant taunt.

Violet threw up her hands. "All right. I will. *Sex.* That's what we had. That's *all* we had."

"See, that wasn't so hard, was it?"

"It would not take much effort to learn to hate you, Slow Larkin."

He made a low sound, as if to let her know that her hatred of him was of little, if any, consequence. "You were saying—about sex," he went on relentlessly.

She raised her chin. "I've said it."

"That all we had together was sex?"

"Yes."

"Funny. That's not what you called it then. Then you called it—" She knew what he was going to say. Love.

She cut him off before he uttered that word, which at the moment seemed infinitely more dangerous than talk of sex could ever be. "I was twenty-one years old. I was...inexperienced."

He shrugged, and she breathed a sigh of guilty relief as she realized he was going to let the subject of love go by without further comment. He went on, "You're saying I seduced you, is that it?"

"No, I am not saying that. I didn't do anything I didn't want to do."

He nodded, conceding her a point in a game to which only he knew the rules. "One for you, Red. I never would have thought you'd admit that."

She forged ahead. "Look. What matters is that we were never right for each other. It would have ended in disaster if I'd gone away with you."

"Or so your old man told you."

"I take responsibility for my actions. It was my decision."

He said nothing, and his silence, from the dim end of the couch, seemed damning.

"So that *is* it, then?" she asked when she could bear the quiet no more. "After all these years, you still want revenge on me for breaking my promise to you?"

He said nothing.

She marched over to him and planted herself squarely before him. "Answer me, damn it! Let's have it out in the open, at least."

She watched that lazy grin spread across his face. "You're making a big issue out of nothing, Red."

"It is *not* nothing. You've invaded my home, and you're...lying in wait for me every time I turn around. It's some kind of sick revenge, admit it. Just admit it, damn you!"

He stood then, with that shadowy ease that unnerved her at the same time it drew her. She fell back; she'd learned her lesson after what had happened a few minutes ago. It just didn't pay to let him get too close.

His eyes narrowed a little as he saw the way she shrank from him. Then he shrugged. "Your imagination's working overtime. I'm here to give Lacy Jay a new start in a safe town. That's all."

"Liar," she said softly.

His jaw tightened at that, and she realized she'd struck a telling blow. When he spoke, it was with deadly softness. "Let's not start calling each other names, Red. It's not a good idea, considering that we're going to be seeing so much of each other for a while."

"How long?" she demanded, her voice edged in desperation. "How long are you going to be taking over my house?"

He rubbed his chin thoughtfully, making a cruel taunt of thinking it over. "Well, let's see..."

"Yes?"

"I'll need to find a garage so I can set up a shop first."

"Why?"

He pretended to look reproachful again. "I need a place to work first, choosing a house is secondary."

"That's ridiculous. You own a *corporation* in Southern California, for heaven's sake. Don't try to convince me that you'll go broke if you don't immediately open up a garage and start fooling around under people's hoods."

She saw the little quirk at the edge of his mouth that meant he was trying to keep from laughing. "*Fooling around*—that's how you see my life's work?"

Violet wanted to scream again. "All right. Fine. If you have to find a place to work first, that's what you have to do. Just...give it to me straight. How long are you going to be staying in my house?"

"Well..." He made her wait one more time, and then he grudgingly allowed, "Let's say a month. Tops."

"A *month?*" Violet groaned.

The weeks stretched out ahead of her, an emotional battlefield of verbal warfare and sexual tension.

"Don't worry, Red," he blithely advised, "I'm sure after a few days of getting comfortable with each other's habits, we'll learn to get along just fine."

"A month?" she asked again, trying to accept the enormity of it. What if she ended up killing him—or worse, attacking him in his bed and demanding that he make slow, incredible love to her as only he knew how?

"And who knows?" he added. "Maybe Lacy Jay and I'll be out of here in three weeks if things move right along."

"Terrific," she muttered and had to rub her eyes again. They were beginning to burn now. She needed to take out her contacts. Her headache was worse, squeezing her temples in a tightening band.

It was time, she confessed silently, to concede the field. For the day. She needed a good night's sleep. Perhaps, come tomorrow, she'd think of a way to get rid of this full-grown delinquent who alternately taunted her, insulted her and drove her wild with desire.

"I am going to bed," she said flatly, scooping up her shoes and turning to take her bag from the top of the television. "Good night." She trudged through the arch into the dining room.

"Night, Red," he said, when she was almost through the door to the pantry. The two words were soft, and full of something that made no sense at all—something that might have been fondness, or even tenderness. Which, of course, was impossible. If she'd learned one thing tonight, it was that Slow Larkin bore her little, if any, fondness.

Violet decided her exhausted mind was playing tricks on her. She kept moving, and neither answered nor turned back.

After she was gone, Slow reclaimed her father's chair and picked up his magazine again. But the article he'd been reading had lost interest for him. He reached for the remote, turned on the TV and began flicking the channels, hardly noticing the changing images before him.

He was feeling good. He was feeling *terrific*, as a matter of fact. Red might have stomped on his heart all those years ago, but tonight she hadn't let him down. She'd been unable to commit herself to Darrell Carruthers. Whether she was willing to admit it in words or not, she didn't really want to share her future with the other man. In taking his revenge, Slow wouldn't be destroying anything for her, except maybe her defenses and her self-control.

Slow chuckled softly, thinking about her, about the way she curled her toes when he looked at them, and about the sad little sag to her shoulders as she'd plodded off to bed.

It wasn't even ten yet, he thought with a rueful smile, but she'd be asleep before her head hit the pillow. Beyond her weariness after all that had happened today, Red was a day person. Slow himself never went to bed before two, while Violet liked to slide between the covers well before the witching hour and be up with the sun come morning.

During that week eleven years ago, they used to kid each other about that: a day person and a night person—how would they ever make it work?

Answer: they hadn't.

With a little help from her father, she'd decided that what she and Slow had shared was no more than sex. And as she'd said herself tonight, sex wasn't enough.

Slow grunted, and switched to another channel.

Maybe, he thought with grim satisfaction, sex wasn't enough to make a relationship work. But it was damn well going to make his revenge work just fine.

From what he'd seen in her eyes tonight, when all he'd done was lay his hand on her throat, it was going to be very sweet—to break down all the barriers she had against him again, and make her face that side of herself that she'd spent so much of her life trying to deny. Inside Violet Anne Windemere was a full-blown, sensual woman who longed for Slow Larkin's touch. Slow intended to make sure that the woman got loose.

However, she was going to be more wary of letting him get close after tonight. Bad Slow Larkin had put his hand on her, and she'd almost lost control. She'd be on her guard after this, jumping out of reach like a spooked doe if he got too near. He wouldn't be able to touch her again until he got her to relax a little with him.

The next step, he decided, was going to be to make her trust him, to ease off on the verbal assaults and work on developing some kind of friendly rapport between them. She would never come to him willingly unless she learned to like him as well as want him.

From outside he heard a faraway rumbling sound. Thunder. A summer storm must be coming in. He

smiled, thinking of Lacy. She'd be disappointed if tomorrow's promised trip to the fair was ruined by rain.

The thunder rumbled again, and Slow stood and
walked to the window. He pulled the curtains aside
and looked up at the sky. He saw no stars, which
meant heavy clouds. Then the sky was split by light-
ning, followed by thunder again, echoing the sudden
brightness with sound. When the sound faded, he realized again how damned quiet the old house was.

He considered the heavy silence of the house,
weighing it in his mind. What must it be like for Red,
he wondered, to live here alone? Was it lonely? Did
she, maybe, wish for the sound of other voices, of
laughter and other footsteps besides her own on the
stairs?

"A big house, Slow," she had told him during their
one week of love. "A big, cluttered house with ten kids
and six dogs and lots of noise and laughter. That's
what we'll have, okay? Nothing like what *we* had when
we were growing up. Our kids won't be *only* kids. Our
kids will have brothers and sisters. And all the racket
all the time will drive us nuts, but we'll love it anyway
because we'll know we've got everything that counts
in the world...."

Slow grinned at his own dark reflection in the window glass. That was an idea. He could liven this old
tomb up a little, make friends with her neighbors and
get Glory and that boyfriend of hers to start hanging
around. Violet would moan and complain that he was
way out of line, turning her house into Grand Central
Station, but underneath she'd love it. He was sure of
that.

A sharp gust of wind blew the first drops of rain against the window. Out on the lawn, the rotary sprinkler head spun.

Slow stared at the sprinkler, making a mental note that she still watered the yard by moving a hose around. It would be a hell of a lot more convenient for her to just set the timer on an automatic sprinkler system and let it do the work. For Slow, who'd always been good with his hands, installing such a system wouldn't take more than a day or two.

Playing handyman was definitely a thought. Though the place was excellently maintained, there were still probably a hundred things he could do around here to make life a little easier for her.

He grunted. The old cliché went that the way to a man's heart was through his stomach. Slow wondered why there wasn't a similar saying about the way into a woman's bed: *look handy, and carry a big screwdriver....*

Slow went ahead and laughed out loud at the image the phrase created in his mind. Then he fell silent again as the rain began to pelt the window in earnest.

Chapter Six

Violet woke the next morning feeling rejuvenated.

She stretched luxuriously and let out a lusty sigh. Then she lay still under the sheets, becoming aware of the soft plopping sounds outside the window that meant rainwater was dripping from the eaves to wet ground below. Violet grinned a little, thinking that a rainy Sunday in the middle of August was somewhat of a novelty and thus to be enjoyed.

Then she frowned, staring up at the ceiling as she perceived anew that she would not be enjoying this particular Sunday alone. Slow Larkin would be here—for this and very likely the next four Sundays running.

"Argh!" Violet rolled over and groaned facedown into her pillow before sitting up and throwing back the covers.

She hung there, on the edge of the bed, looking down at her bare toes for a while, thinking. And when she looked up, she was smiling again.

"So what?" she announced defiantly to her cozy little room.

He was here, and there wasn't much she'd been able to do about it. She was just going to have to live with it for a month. That was hardly a lifetime, after all. Even if he did everything in his power to make her life a living hell while he stayed here, he would eventually be gone. And in the end, it was her choice how she reacted to the things he did anyway.

Violet felt totally invigorated. In fact, looked at from the fresh perspective of a good night's sleep, all the confusions of the day before now seemed what she was sure they'd actually been: a sort of odd emotional aberration brought on by the shock of seeing Slow again after all these years. This morning, after a night of much-needed rest during which her subconscious mind had had time to digest the fact that he was back, she was going to find that he didn't really affect her at all anymore. Not the least little bit. She was sure of it.

With that thought firmly in mind, Violet jumped from the bed and went straight to the bathroom. She splashed refreshing water on her face and swiftly brushed her sleep-tangled hair.

Obviously, she thought, those incredible sensations that had seemed to take control of her, sensations that had felt so overpowering yesterday and last night, had never really been there at all. They were a throwback, that was all, to another time when she'd been younger and not nearly so wise.

Violet went back to her room to dress and make her bed. As she tucked in the sheets and smoothed the lace-edged comforter, she came to another blinding awareness: there was absolutely no reason for her to toss out her carefully considered decision to marry Darrell just because Slow Larkin had decided to pop back into her life and drive her crazy for the next month or so.

She and Darrell already had a date for tonight; she was invited to the farewell dinner he was cooking for his parents at his house. Tomorrow Darrell, Sr. and Joyce Carruthers were leaving in their travel trailer for an extended stay in the Sawtooth Mountains of Idaho. More than likely Violet would have ample opportunity sometime during the evening to tell Darrell what she should have told him last night.

But then again, why wait until tonight? Why not just call him right after breakfast?

With three decisive flicks of her wrist, Violet tossed the embroidered throw pillows against the headboard. Yes, that was what she would do. She would call Darrell after breakfast and tell him *yes* right there on the phone, and that would be that. Slow Larkin or no Slow Larkin, she was getting on with her life.

Violet turned and marched resolutely to the kitchen, where she found Lacy Jay reading the back of a cornflakes box. The child looked up at the sound Violet's footsteps and a big, happy smile spread across her face.

"Oh, wow, great. Someone who gets up early. I can get used to that. Dad never gets up before noon. I *loathe* eating breakfast alone."

Violet chuckled. "*Loathe* is a pretty strong word for so early in the morning."

"Yeah. Ain't it great? Glory said it and I asked her about it. We looked it up. It's like really, really hating something with complete and total disgust. The Wordman would love that."

"The Wordman?" Violet echoed rather blankly, moving to the counter to load up the coffeemaker.

"The Wordman." Lacy Jay launched into an explanation without further prompting. "He lives in the vacant lot at the end of our street in North Hollywood, in a tent. He has a dog named Miser and about ten dictionaries and lots of people say he's just a crazy bum. But he's not, he's my friend. He's Dad's friend, too. Dad's always trying to give him a job. But the Wordman says he's not the type to labor and be heavy burdened. He says his tent is roof enough for him and he lives on the fruits of the mind."

"He does?" Violet said, not really knowing what else to say.

"I used to laugh about that," Lacy Jay rambled on. "You know, him having fruit in his head. That sounded pretty weird to me. But when I got a little older, I found out that fruits of the mind are like your thoughts."

Violet made a noise of assent and nodded somewhat absently. She was only half listening to the girl at that moment. She was wondering again about the life Slow and Lacy had left behind, an odd kind of life, it sounded like, but one that seemed to have suited them. Also Lacy Jay's chatter told her a little more about Slow.

He'd offered a homeless man a job. It was further evidence, beyond his taking full responsibility for raising a daughter, that there was more to him than the overgrown bad boy he'd been playing with a vengeance since yesterday afternoon.

However, Violet scolded herself, the many sides of Slow Larkin were not her concern.

Putting him firmly from her mind, Violet turned from the counter to see Lacy Jay peeling open the cornflakes box. "How about some eggs?" Violet asked.

Lacy Jay screwed up her nose in an expression that seemed to mean she was giving the question serious thought. "You gonna make scrambled?"

"Do you want scrambled?"

"Yeah."

"Okay, then. Scrambled it is."

Lacy Jay set the kitchen table for two as Violet fixed the food. They sat down together and Violet heard more about North Hollywood, about Wordman and Miser and Madame Albondiga, who lived in an apartment the next street over and told fortunes at reasonable rates.

When the eggs were eaten, Lacy Jay helped clean up. After that, Violet was going to call Darrell—she really was—but somehow she and Lacy Jay wandered into the living room together and Lacy Jay stood at the window looking out, bemoaning the rain that would keep Glorianna from taking her to the fair.

"And this is the last day, too. Glory told me yesterday that we'd be sure to go today because we wouldn't have another chance."

Violet put off her call to Darrell to sympathize with Lacy Jay. And then they went out, sharing an umbrella, to feed the goldfish in the pond behind the house. When they came back in, they were laughing and damp and Violet poured herself another cup of coffee while Lacy Jay went into the living room to turn on the television.

Violet wandered back into the dining room, thinking she could make her call now. But then Lacy Jay heard her coming and looked up from where she was stretched on the rug and asked a question—and they were off and talking and laughing again.

Somehow the time just melted away. And then, near noon, Glorianna and Arthur arrived. Violet and Lacy Jay went to the door to let them in from the rain.

They were all standing in the entry hall in a welcoming knot, prior to filing back into the living room, when Violet half consciously became aware of movement at the top of the stairs.

She looked up before the others and saw Slow standing there, his hand on the railing, looking down.

And the true understanding of the predicament she was in dropped on her—like something huge and heavy falling out of the sky, knocking breath, thought and everything else right out of her.

His eyes were still heavy with recent sleep, his hair was mussed. He wore only his black jeans and his rogue's smile as his eyes locked with hers.

"Mornin', Red." He more mouthed the words than said them.

Violet stared up at him, unable to do anything else right then, even incapable of masking the blank, trapped desperation that had taken hold of her like a numbing drug.

Meanwhile, in her midsection, heat was curling, just like her toes were doing inside her tennis shoes.

I want him, she thought in a kind of wretched wonder. I want him with the same overwhelming heat and intensity as I did years ago. It's starting all over again. Just like before.

How could she have been such a silly fool this morning, to merrily assume that the cravings he'd roused in her yesterday had only been echoes of what once was?

The way her skin prickled and yearned all over; the deep, hard beating of her heart; the way her breasts ached, the nipples suddenly feeling hard and sensitive—those were no echoes. Those sensations were real. And her blithe arrogance in believing her responses yesterday had only been an overactive imagination, that was a lie.

From the top of the stairs, Slow's blue eyes licked over her, somewhat possessively, she thought. It was as if he knew how easy it was all going to be, now that he was in her house, to get into her bed.

"Dad, you're up!" Lacy Jay called, spotting him then. He shrugged, one bare shoulder lifting and lowering in a movement that seemed pure poetry to Violet, who had to restrain herself from actually licking her lips.

"Did I have a choice?" he teased sleepily. "Sounds like an opening night at Mann's Chinese Theater down here." He started down the stairs, and Violet forced her gaze away from the sight of him coming ever nearer.

The gray day outside now seemed to have taken up residence in her heart as she accepted the repercussions of her own emotions: there was no way she could call Darrell now.

Until she'd resolved these tortuous feelings about Slow, she could never go on with her plans to marry her lifelong friend and start a family of her own with him. Hungering after Slow as she was right now, her wedding night would be the kind of disaster no man or woman should ever be forced to live through.

Numbly Violet allowed herself to be borne along with the others back into the living room. There, Glorianna handed Lacy Jay a bag with a local video rental's logo emblazoned on it.

"Something to while away a rainy day," Glorianna suggested.

"Glory, I *loathe* cartoons," Lacy Jay announced when she glanced at the titles.

Violet, ever so painfully aware of Slow, hesitated to see where he would position himself in the room—in order that she could find a place as far away from him as possible. When he moved to stand behind the couch, she backed toward the hall again and stood against the arch that separated it from the living room. He gave her a quick, sharp glance—a glance that turned her knees to jelly, seeming to speak as it did of the impossibility of her ever really escaping him.

"You're only nine, my sweet," Glorianna declared grandly. "Much too young to *loathe* anything—but if you dislike cartoons, then what *do* you enjoy?"

"Horror," Lacy Jay responded without missing a beat.

Glorianna indulged in an effusive shudder. "You mean bodies and blood and chain saws and all of that?"

Lacy Jay hoisted herself up on the couch, shucked off her boots and crossed her legs Indian-style. Then she paused to consider, her expression turning slightly crafty. "Why? Can we go trade these in on some horror movies?"

Slow, still standing behind the couch, interrupted the exchange by putting his hands on his daughter's shoulders. "You know the rules on this. Tell Glory."

Lacy Jay made a sour face but then conceded. "Oh, all right. No movies with people getting cut up or slashed to pieces. And no movies with exploding heads."

Glorianna looked slightly bewildered. "Exploding heads?"

"Yeah, we rented this one movie once where I swore to Dad that the picture on the box was fine, nobody getting cut up or anything. And that was true. But there *was* a picture of a guy's head exploding. And then the movie turned out to be pretty grotesque, actually. So from then on we had the exploding heads rule." Lacy looked up at her father and grinned. "Right?"

Slow squeezed her shoulders. "Right."

Violet, watching from her safe distance across the room, saw the special quality of the look that passed between father and daughter. It was a look of shared experience, a look of compromises made and mutual tolerance—and love.

She was reminded, once again, of what an attentive, caring father Slow was proving to be—and that made her feel doubly frustrated. He was so contradictory—subtly tormenting Violet one minute, and then smiling down at his daughter in love and frank understanding the next.

"So can we go back to the video store, Glory?" Lacy Jay's request brought Violet's attention back to the subject at hand.

"Certainly. Put your boots back on and get a light jacket."

Within minutes, Glorianna, Arthur and Lacy Jay were on their way outside. Violet and Slow somehow ended up in the hall together waving goodbye and closing the door.

They stood for a moment, when the house was quiet again, very close but not touching. Violet was sure he must be able to hear her heart, which felt as if it was pounding almost hard enough to crack her ribs. She was trying not to look at his bare chest, which had dark hair whorling on it in a T-shaped pattern—out over his little nipples and then along the center of his hard belly.

Violet realized she was following that tempting trail of hair downward to where it disappeared beneath the buttons of his jeans—and jerked her head up. Blue eyes shone at her, hot and full of something that looked like triumph for a fraction of a second.

She had a sinking, surrendering feeling, an incredibly voluptuous hollowing out down inside her. She waited, thinking he would touch her, and that it was inevitable anyway—why fight it?

Still, something else in her held out, refused to sway the slight distance it would have taken to bring her soft body into contact with his.

On stiff legs, she stepped back.

And watching her movement, his eyes changed. He veiled them.

Then he said, "I need a cup of coffee," in a completely neutral voice and turned for the kitchen. She had to force herself not to stare hungrily at the tight movement of his buttocks as he lazily sauntered away.

The rest of the day was much the same. Violet tried her best to keep her distance, and strangely, after that near miss at the front door, Slow seemed to go along.

This made her more confused and edgy than ever. She began to doubt a little that he still felt the same hungers she did.

Surprisingly, though, the rainy day proceeded rather enjoyably on the whole, with everybody ensconced in the living room munching the pretzels and trail mix that Glorianna had provided and watching Vincent Price lure a series of sweet young things to his gloomy castle.

Then after the first of the series of movies they'd rented was over, Glorianna decided they should make a horror story of their own. The endlessly agreeable Arthur was sent out to buy crayons and glue and construction paper and, with the succession of scary videos providing inspiration, Glorianna and Lacy Jay created an illustrated book, *Blood City,* about a group of preteen vampires from Hollywood set loose in a small Northern California town.

Violet watched her mother and Slow's child, their heads close together as they labored over the bright papers spread out on the living room rug. She couldn't help remembering her own childhood when her mother was forever inventing ways to make the day-to-day world seem full of magic and wonder. Her father, back then, had called it "pure foolishness."

"This is pure foolishness, Glorianna," he would say gruffly. "Drawing pictures and making up stories and playing dress up with her every chance you get. Violet Anne's time would be much better spent learning something useful— What is six times seven, Violet Anne? Right now. You shouldn't even need to think about it..."

On the floor, Lacy Jay crowed in delight at some new twist Glorianna had added to the story. A smile tugging on her own lips, Violet looked up—and found Slow, who seemed to have laid permanent claim to her father's big chair, sitting there watching her.

Violet stared right back at him, wondering again what was going on in his head. But his expression revealed nothing. After a moment, he looked away as he stood.

"Anyone want another soda?" he asked over his shoulder and headed through the dining room in the direction of the kitchen. There were no takers as he disappeared into the butler's pantry.

Violet tried to bring her attention back to the open file folder in her lap. The folder represented a personal injury case for which she was taking the opposing client's deposition the next day. She had a small stack of similar folders on the table beside her and she'd been leisurely reviewing what was coming up on her calendar tomorrow.

Perhaps, she thought wryly, she would have been smarter to work in her room where there would have been no distractions—or even to drive the few blocks to the offices she and Darrell shared with four other attorneys. But it was so pleasant sitting here in the living room with the warm summer rain drumming on the windows while Lacy Jay and Glorianna giggled together on the floor and Arthur sat on the other end of the couch deep in concentration over the Sunday crossword puzzle.

Violet jumped as the telephone on the side table in the dining room rang. She set the folder on top of the stack beside her and went to pick it up, realizing just before she said hello that it had stopped ringing before she got there.

She knew why a moment later. Slow had picked up the kitchen extension.

"That you, Red?" his voice drawled in her ear.

"Yes."

"Good. It's for you."

"Thank you." She waited for him to get off the line.

"Nice talkin' to you there, Darrell," Slow added.

Suddenly the silence from the third presence on the line seemed ominous.

"Slow. You can hang up now," Violet said in measured tones.

"Right. You take real good care of yourself, Darrell."

Darrell didn't deign to respond. At last there was the click that signified Slow had hung up.

"Darrell?"

"Yes, I'm here." His voice was very controlled.

Violet opened her mouth to say something appeasing, and then changed her mind as Slow materialized in the doorway of the pantry. He would hear anything she said about him now and, knowing him, that would probably only serve to encourage him.

"Just calling to remind you about tonight," Darrell said, giving her the cue that he, too, would prefer to leave the subject of Slow Larkin and his rudeness behind.

Violet hardly heard the next thing Darrell said because she was so overly conscious of Slow. Instead of allowing her a minimum of privacy for her conversation, he had suddenly decided to lurk directly in her line of vision. He leaned forward, one arm braced against the door frame. Then he tipped his head back for a long swig from the frosty can of soda he held. Violet watched his strong neck move as the soda slid down his throat. He swallowed like he did everything else—with a kind of laid-back gusto that she found infuriatingly seductive.

Fascinated with just watching him swallow, she bleakly told herself she should be grateful for small favors. After his first cup of coffee, he'd at least had the courtesy to put on a T-shirt. A white one for a change. It made the skin of his neck and arms look nut brown. Also, now that she was staring at him, Violet noticed that even though his chest was covered the strong shape of it was clearly delineated beneath the clinging cotton of the shirt...

"Violet, are you there?"

"Yes—yes, Darrell. I'm here."

In the doorway, Slow had lowered the can of soda and was aiming one of those lazy, insolent grins her way.

"All right, then," Darrell said. "Can you be here by six?"

"Six?"

"My parents won't be here until seven. Dinner's at eight."

Violet remembered. The farewell dinner. For Darrell's parents.

"It's Oriental chicken with soya cream sauce over fresh linguine," Darrell went on. He was an amateur gourmet chef.

"Sounds delicious," Violet said.

Slow took another pull at his soda, and then tipped the can at her in a sort of cocky salute. He straightened from his slouch against the door frame and strolled back into the living room to join the others.

Violet caught herself staring after his retreating backside—a practice that could become a habit if she didn't watch herself like a hawk.

"So if you could just pick it up on your way, it would be great," Darrell was saying.

"Excuse me. What did you say, Darrell?"

"Arugula. I need a head of arugula for a garnish. Is there something distracting you? I'm sure I spoke clearly the first time." Darrell sounded suddenly curt.

"I apologize, Darrell," Violet said evenly. "You're right, I wasn't paying as much attention as I should have. I'd be happy to pick up the arugula."

"Wonderful," Darrell said after a moment in the tone of a man who knew when to let sleeping dogs lie. "And you're sure you don't mind?"

"Of course not. Six o'clock, then?"

"Terrific. Six o'clock."

Violet hung up and returned to the living room, where Slow was now assisting Lacy Jay and Glorianna in getting the preteen vampires out of yet another sticky situation.

The oddly pleasurable rainy day continued as it had been until a little after five, when all but Violet piled into Slow's black Chevy and headed for the Citizen's Restaurant on Broad Street for pizza with the works. Later, since Glorianna had secured the tickets, they would be taking in a performance at the local Performing Arts Center Theatre.

After they left, Violet had to rush to get ready for dinner at Darrell's and still save time to pick up the produce he'd asked for. When she arrived at his house, she helped him set the table and fix the salad.

The dinner went off nicely, and the decadent black-forest cake Darrell served for dessert was the perfect finishing touch to an otherwise light meal. By nine, the elder Carrutherses were saying goodbye and promising their son that they'd check in regularly from Idaho, as well as send postcards by the score.

"I'll just help you carry the plates back to the kitchen," Violet said when they were alone.

But Darrell waved that suggestion away, reminding her that dishes were one of the reasons he had a housekeeper come in three times a week. "Come into the living room," he coaxed.

She followed reluctantly, into the large, octagonal space that was furnished in neutral colors—tans and grays, mostly, with occasional touches of muted red. Darrell gestured at the tan couch. Violet sat down, and then he sat beside her.

He put his arm along the back of the couch behind her, and she instinctively shied out of the circle it made. But then she thought of Slow's taunting jibe the night before: "You *tolerated* his touch. Body language. It tells so much..."

Defiantly Violet forced herself to lean back into the circle of Darrell's arm—and it felt all wrong.

This just isn't going to work, she thought. And knew it was only fair to let Darrell off the hook for good and all.

She straightened. "Darrell..."

He looked at her, his eyes full of devotion. "Yes, darling."

Violet swallowed and pulled back a little more. "Darrell, I have something to say..."

"All right."

She clutched her hands together in her lap and launched herself into the waiting silence between them. The words came out stiffly, and yet they tumbled over one another at the same time.

"I'm having...some really confusing feelings, since yesterday, since Slow arrived at my door. And the nature of these feelings is such that I really don't think it's fair to you to keep you dangling like this."

Darrell looked at her for a moment, and Violet found it impossible to figure out what was going through his mind. Then he very deliberately put his hand over hers. She stiffened but didn't pull away because his grip was rather firm—she would have had to draw back violently to escape it. She felt she was hurting him enough without jerking away from him as if he repulsed her.

"Darling, please don't be so hasty about this."

"Darrell, I know this is the right thing to do. It's better to—"

He stopped her from finishing her thought. "No, it's not," he said firmly. "As you said yourself, you're confused. It's completely unwise to make a decision like this when you're confused."

Violet found the will to extricate her hand from his. "Don't patronize me, Darrell. I may be confused but I'm not mentally incompetent."

He looked at her for a moment as if he doubted the truth of that last statement, and then he changed tactics on her. "If you won't agree to marry me, will you do one thing for me?"

She stood and paced around the huge gray marble coffee table to the wall of windows on the west side of the room. In the daytime the windows looked out on an attractively landscaped yard rimmed in pine trees and a slope that led to a creek behind the house. But now, at night, all Violet saw was her own pensive reflection and the neutral-colored room surrounding her.

She turned back to the man who sat on the couch. "It's just not right, Darrell. It just...doesn't feel right anymore."

"All right. I understand—"

"I don't think you do. I don't think you—"

"Just let me finish. Just let me say what I have to say." He looked at her, and there was plain adoration in his eyes.

Always—all their lives—it seemed Darrell had been looking at her like that, with an adoring kind of love that she couldn't return in kind but that somehow made her feel protective toward him at the same time. Darrell's worshipful love had always bewildered her, as her own desire for Slow Larkin bewildered her. It had been her father's dream that she would one day marry Darrell, and she knew Darrell's parents hoped for the same thing. And that had always been just fine with Darrell because Darrell wanted it, too, had always wanted it, no matter how many times Violet had gently told him no.

Now confronted once again with the baffling intensity of Darrell's feelings for her, Violet heard herself acquiescing. "All right, Darrell. What is it you want to say?"

He was quiet for a moment more, as if to be sure he had her attention. Then he said, "If you can't say yes, then just don't say no. At least until that man is out of your house and you're yourself again."

"Darrell, he could be there a *month*..."

Darrell blinked at that, and she could see he found the prospect of Slow Larkin in residence for weeks on end just as daunting as she did. But then he drew in a breath and said, "It doesn't matter. You know it doesn't. What's another month to me after I've already waited for half a lifetime?"

Violet looked down at the floor and then back up at him. "It isn't right—"

He knew she was weakening and he forged ahead. "We won't bring it up again. We'll put you and me on 'hold,' so to speak—unless you'll occasionally agree to dinner or a show—until Slow Larkin has been out of your house for a week. And then we'll see how you feel."

"I don't know, Darrell—"

"And who knows, maybe he'll suddenly decide to get out tomorrow or the next day."

There was a funny note in his voice. Violet glanced at him sharply. "What would make him decide to do that?" He looked away. "Darrell, I meant what I said last night. I want you to stay out of it."

"Of course." He looked back at her levelly. "I promised I would, didn't I?"

"Then what makes you say—"

"Well, anything's possible with him, isn't it?"

"Yes. Yes, you're right about that."

"So perhaps his unpredictability will end up working in our favor."

"That's certainly possible."

He stood, and his lips curved in a guileless, open smile. "So do we have an agreement, then? Not a yes—but not a no, either, until the source of your...confusion is gone?"

Violet looked at him, and then said bluntly, "Maybe it just isn't meant to be between you and me, did you ever think of that?"

His expression darkened. "It's always been meant to be," he said, his stubborn jaw tensing. "And we'd be engaged right now if it wasn't for that bastard who won't leave you alone."

"Darrell, I don't think—"

But he didn't want to hear. "Please. It's all I'm asking. Just don't say no until after he's out of your life again."

"Darrell..."

"Please."

Violet sighed. "All right, Darrell. We'll talk about it once more, after Slow's gone."

Chapter Seven

"Dad?"

Lacy's coaxing voice brought Slow up from that hazy place between a dream and consciousness. His head still buried in the pillow, he mumbled, "Wha—huh?"

"You said to wake you up before I left. I made coffee."

Just as she said the word coffee, Slow became aware of the tempting aroma. Definitely coffee.

He rolled his head toward his daughter and pried open one eye. "You always did know how to work me."

Lacy beamed at him. "It's fresh. I watched Violet make it and I copied her."

Slow hauled himself upright against the headboard and Lacy Jay handed over the steaming mug. He sipped.

"Liquid heaven," he said. "What time is it?"

"Eleven-thirty."

"Violet already gone?"

"Yep. She left at about eight. We had breakfast together. Glory'll be here in a few minutes to get me."

Slow still wasn't fully awake. "She will?"

Lacy put on her I'm-patient-with-all-idiots-and-parents voice. "Dad. Remember? Glory's making me lunch and then we're going swimming at the condo."

The cobwebs of sleep cleared some more and he recalled the arrangements they'd made the night before. "Right. I remember." Lacy looked at him doubtfully, and he found himself repeating, "I do. I remember."

"Good. I'll be back by five." Downstairs the door chimes rang. "That's her." Lacy Jay scrambled up beside him and planted a kiss on his unshaven cheek. "Love you."

Slow grunted.

Lacy bounded off the bed and headed for the stairs.

"Lace?"

She turned, a slight figure in black jeans and T-shirt, her only ornament a leather bracelet with steel studs. She'd gotten into the mousse or something, and her hair was slicked down and stuck together in the style of those old Latin lovers of the silent screen.

"Love your hair," he said.

"Aw, Dad..."

"Love you, too."

She gave him a smile that showed all her teeth and was gone.

Slow sat in Clovis Windemere's lumpy old bed, sipped his coffee and listened to the greetings downstairs, the sound of Lacy rushing back up again—

presumably to her room to get her swimsuit—and then her pounding down once more. In no time at all the front door closed and the house was quiet again.

He sat a little longer, enjoying the quiet, thinking that he'd done at least one thing right in his life and that one thing was Lacy Jay. She seemed to be handling the move pretty well so far, too.

Then he drained the last of his coffee and decided he wanted some more. He got up and pulled on jeans and went down to the kitchen, pausing only for a glance out the big upper gallery window.

Outside, the late-morning sky was powder blue, washed clean by yesterday's steady rain. It would be a perfect day to start installing the automatic sprinkler system he'd been thinking about, because the ground would be soft.

If he got started right away, he could probably get the front yard sprinklers in before dark. He grinned, thinking of Red's face when she came home to find that he'd dug up her front yard. She'd be mad, and then bewildered. And then she'd start *reasoning* with him, explaining why he was way out of line and why she couldn't let him do that.

And he'd tell her that it was only his way of showing his appreciation for staying in her house.

And then, whatever happened after that, they would have been *talking* to each other. And that would be a start on getting her to let down her guard a little.

Yesterday had proved to him that making her like him and getting her to open up to him was critical. The little witch virtually quaked with desire every time she looked at him—but she was being damn careful not to let him get too close. He was going to have to take care of that problem—by keeping hands-off for a while, no matter how much he wanted to grab her and put his mouth on hers and show her exactly what she'd been missing since she'd last sent him away.

Slow chuckled to himself. There were advantages, for a man, in not being eighteen anymore. It was just possible, if he exercised every last smidgen of self-control he possessed, that *she* would explode with unsatisfied lust before he did.

Red, after all, was a woman in her thirties. It was tough for women in their thirties. Sexually, women peaked then, from what he understood. Poor Red. Her hormones were really going to be working against her in this situation.

As for himself, well, he was over the hill, sexually speaking. It was easier than it would have been a few years ago for him to hold out against those melting *take-me* looks she kept giving him. And he intended to hold out, until she wanted him so much that she was willing to be the aggressor, to state her desire right out loud—and to prove it in no uncertain terms.

Still grinning, Slow poured his second cup of coffee and went foraging in her kitchen drawers for a pencil and pad to make a list to take to the hardware store. Just as he found what he sought, the door chimes rang again.

Thinking Lacy must have forgotten something and locked herself out, he strolled quickly to the front hall, still carrying his coffee.

He flung the door open to find Darrell Carruthers standing there.

"I want to talk to you," the other man said tightly after a long moment where the two simply stared at each other.

Slow said nothing for a few seconds more while, out on the street, a boy went by on a bicycle, tickers hooked to his spokes so they clicked furiously like a grasshopper gone made.

As the sound of the ticking bicycle faded off down the street, Slow decided that he wasn't surprised—not in finding Darrell on the doorstep, nor in the essentially predictable ways the other man had changed in the past eleven years. He took a leisurely moment to look the other man over, as he hadn't really had the opportunity to do the other night when Darrell came to pick up Violet for dinner.

Darrell Carruthers was a handsome man. More so now that time had worn some hollows in his cheeks and left a few crow's-feet around his pale eyes. Eleven years ago, Darrell's style had been college-boy casual. Now he was that same college boy a decade later, a professional man from head to toe. His gray suit fit too well in the shoulders to have come off a rack, and some cobbler in Italy had no doubt been responsible for his shoes.

Slow suppressed a smile as he felt the damning sweep of the other man's gaze looking *him* over in return. Darrell's barely restrained disgust and impotent anger came at him in waves. Probably, Slow thought with a wicked internal chuckle, he should have thrown on a shirt before answering the door. After all, it couldn't be too pleasant for poor Darrell to find his age-old rival shoeless and shirtless and obviously right at home in Darrell's *almost*-fiancée's house.

"Come on in," Slow said and elaborately moved out of the other man's way. "It just so happens there's nobody here but me."

"I know," Darrell said. "Violet mentioned this morning that your daughter would be with Glori-anna. Swimming or something, I think Violet said."

Slow gave a dry chuckle. "You mean you asked a few subtle questions—to find out when you could catch me alone?"

Darrell's eyes narrowed for a moment, as if he were assessing whether Slow's inquiry was somehow meant to trip him up. Then he shrugged and said, "Yes."

"Red doesn't know you're here, then?"

Darrell winced at Slow's use of the nickname, but apparently decided not to make a big deal of it; he had more pressing issues to tackle. "No," he said, "she doesn't know. This is just between us. Fair enough?"

Slow almost asked what *fair* had ever had to do with anything between the two of them, but decided the remark was futile. He said, "Sure. Why not?" Then he lifted his cup. "Coffee?"

"No, thank you."

"Suit yourself." They moved of a wary accord into the living room. Slow gestured at the couch. "Have a seat."

"I prefer to stand."

Slow shrugged and dropped into the big easy chair in the middle of the room. He hoisted his bare feet up on the ottoman in front of him and took another lei-surely sip from his mug. "So what can I do for you, Darrell?"

Darrell glared at him for a moment. Then he said, "You know very well what you can do. Leave town."

Slow shook his head. "Sorry, Darrell. Can't help you there."

Darrell made an angry sound in his throat, looked toward the turret windows and then back at Slow. "All right. Let's try it from this angle. What do you want here?''

Slow considered the question, thinking briefly of giving the half lie he'd given Violet—that he was looking for a safe place to raise Lacy Jay. But somehow he couldn't bring himself to mention his daughter now. The animosity between himself and Darrell hung in the air, smelling of male-to-male rivalry and ugly betrayal. He didn't want Lacy tainted by it, even in the passing mention of her name to the other man.

"I'll ask you again," Darrell prodded when Slow didn't immediately answer, "in case you didn't hear me just then. What do you want?"

"Hmm..." Slow set his coffee cup on his bare stomach and looked down into it, as if seeking the answer to Darrell's question there. After a moment, he looked up again. "What do you think I want, Darrell?"

"Is it money?" Darrell demanded curtly. "Will money do it?"

Slow shook his head. "Darrell," he chided. "You tried that once, remember? It didn't work. And that was when I barely had two quarters to rub together. What makes you think it's going to work now, when I've got all the bucks I need?"

"Then what *do* you want?" Darrell spoke through clenched teeth in a very subdued voice.

Slow set his coffee aside, leaned on an elbow and actually gave the question some serious thought. What did he want? An invitation to Violet's bed, mostly. But that was between him and Red.

Was there something else? Surprisingly a thought came to him. There *was* something he wanted that only the well-bred, handsome man who stood, rigid with leashed anger, across from him could supply.

Slow answered, "To solve a few old mysteries, for a start."

"Mysteries." Darrell cut his eyes away, and then forced himself to look back at Slow once more. "What mysteries?"

Slow grunted. "Come on, rack your memory. Take a wild guess. If you think hard enough, I'm sure you'll know what mysteries I mean."

"Tell me anyway," Darrell shot back. "Then we'll both know for sure."

"All right." Slow shifted in his chair, slouching deeper into it and folding his hands on his stomach. "Let's start with the night they ran me out of town, fifteen years ago."

"What about it?" A muscle in Darrell's jaw twitched. Slow saw it and knew that Darrell knew *exactly* what about it.

"You set me up that night, didn't you?" Slow said flatly, reliving in his mind once more the way it had been.

It was the night after he'd first kissed Violet, and her father had caught them out on her back porch. Slow had been in disgrace, relegated to his room.

And then the tapping had come, on his window. He'd looked out to find Darrell there, signaling him outside where that damn gorgeous car of Darrell, Sr.'s was waiting, gleaming there, on the curb.

Darrell's father had bought the Corvette new, years before that, and he only took it out on Sundays, to cruise around in. Slow supposed it made Darrell's stoop-shouldered, quiet father feel like a sporty kind of guy when he slipped behind the wheel.

But Slow didn't really care what Darrell's old man got out of owning a vintage 'Vette. What Slow cared about was getting inside it, wrapping one hand around the wheel and palming the stick shift with the other. He wanted to take that baby out on a deserted stretch of highway somewhere. There, with only the moon and stars and pine trees looking on, he wanted to shove her up the gears until the neat small-block fuelie under her hood screamed like a wild thing and tore up the road.

Eighteen-year-old idiot that Slow had been that night, he hadn't even stopped to consider what Darrell might be up to, showing up with the keys to a car that his father never permitted another human being to so much as touch—let alone *drive*.

Darrell had dangled the keys in front of Slow. "Want to try her out?"

Now, fifteen years later, Slow said to the other man, "You wanted to make me pay for what happened between Red and me the night before, didn't you? And you knew damn well I'd be too crazy to get behind the wheel of that 'Vette to ask any questions about why your dad was suddenly giving you the keys. I went riding with you, and you let me get behind the wheel, and then you just happened to suggest if we stopped at a drive-in, you'd go in for shakes. So there I was, sitting, grinning like an idiot in the driver's seat when the patrol car pulled up alongside, without a notion in the world that your father had called the police about his *stolen* 'Vette."

Darrell's pale eyes, which had slid away to study the shade of a Tiffany lamp in the corner, suddenly focused on Slow once more. "What does it matter? That was years ago, and from what I've heard you've done all right for yourself since then.''

"You know, Darrell, I've told myself the same thing for a hell of a long time—that your screwing me over like that was in another life, and that it's nothing to me anymore. I spent a lot of years working like a dog to give my kid a future. For a while, I just plain didn't have the time to go chasing after answers to nagging old questions. But now, well, my business can pretty much run itself. Now I got the time.

"And when I heard you and Red might just be tyin' the knot, I suddenly got the motivation. Whatever bad feelings there might be between her and me, I'd just hate to see her hooking herself up to a liar and a cheat.''

Darrell made an outraged noise. "You're trying to tell me you're concerned about Violet? Don't make me laugh.''

Slow shrugged. "Think what you want. But what I'd really like to know now, Darrell, is...did you sneak out the back that night because you were too damned scared to take the rap? Or because you'd actually set me up from the first?''

Darrell cleared his throat, twice.

Slow chuckled, a rather ugly sound, and decided he might as well clear up *both* the old questions at once. "Don't answer yet, Darrell," he said in the tone of a crafty salesman who'd decided to throw in a bonus just to round out the deal. "Let's go on to four years later, first—when I came back to bury my old man, and you saw Red and me together. You swore, when Red asked you to, that you'd say nothing to her father and let us tell him in our own way. Then you snuck over to see me on the sly and offered me money to get out of her life. I took a pass on that.

"And then what do you know? That very night, when she was with me, who shows up but her old man—who takes one look at his precious baby wearing nothing but a sheet with bad Slow Larkin standing right there beside her in his B.V.D.s—and just about has a massive coronary.

"That was not the way we planned to break the news to him. You hear what I'm saying? Somebody told the old bastard, Darrell. Could that somebody have been you?"

"You were bad for her," Darrell muttered tightly and evasively. "You've always been bad for her. Why can't you just get out and stay out? Go back where you belong."

"Come on, Darrell. Let's have it right out there on the table this time. You know damn well I'll never rat on you. I learned early not to bother. I took the rap alone fifteen years ago and never said a word about how I got my hands on the keys to that 'Vette. And I never told Red you offered me money to leave her alone. Guys like me figure it out early that ratting gets us nowhere—nobody ever believes what we say anyway."

"That's because you're not to be trusted," Darrell said through clenched teeth. "You're a snake in the grass."

"Just clear up the old mysteries, Darrell. Just lay it out there on the line. Did you purposely set me up with the Corvette—and did you tell Clovis Windemere about Red and me four years later?"

The two men stared at each other for a moment, neither moving. Then Darrell's eyes acquired a crafty gleam. Slyly he asked, "What will it get me, to give you an answer? Will you leave town once you know?"

Slow laughed, tossing his head toward the ceiling and letting the sound ring out. In spite of its vigor, the laugh had no humor in it. "Sure, Darrell. I'll just pack my bags and head for the door."

"You're lying." Darrell sneered in immediate response.

"You're really sharp, you know that, Darrell?"

"I want you out of town. Today."

"I'm sure you do—but unfortunately there's not a hell of a lot you can pull to get rid of me this time. Old Clovis is dead, so you can't go running to him. And I think I'll just pass on any rides in vintage 'Vettes that you might offer me. You could try planting drugs in my car or having me picked up on some trumped-up charge—but even if you've considered that, you know damn well how tough it would be to make something like that stick. And, besides, you also know that if you're not careful, you just might make me angry enough that I'd decide to tell Red about the various ways you've gotten rid of me over the years."

Darrell puffed out his chest and intoned self-righteously, "She'd never believe you over me."

Slow grinned and recrossed his bare feet on the ottoman. "So. She *doesn't* know. I always wondered about that."

Darrell's eyes slid away again, and he shifted his weight from one foot to the other—a minute movement, but one that Slow didn't miss. Slow knew the other man was beginning to realize he'd made a substantial tactical error: he'd underestimated his rival.

By most definitions of the word, Darrell was a successful man—a lawyer, a pillar of the local community. Over the years, he had no doubt become accustomed to stating his will and having lesser men bow to it. He'd come here to confront the troubled delinquent he'd known years ago, simply assuming that no-good Slow Larkin would end up listening to reason—or veiled threats, if reason failed.

But sadly for Darrell, things weren't working out as he'd planned. Slow wasn't budging—and Darrell had made a major slip and revealed heretofore hidden information to the opposing side. Slow savored the other man's blunder, turning over in his mind the knowledge that Red remained innocent of what Darrell had done.

"Leave her alone, Slow," Darrell said then, his voice suddenly dripping with nobility and wounded dignity. "Leave her alone. *Please.* You've never been anything but trouble for her anyway. I plan to marry her, and to share with her the kind of life she deserves."

Slow's stomach tightened, and he warned himself to stay cool.

But, God, he'd always hated the kind of cheap shot Darrell was pulling now. Slow hated the way Darrell could fight so damned dirty, stab you in the back and do it cheerfully—and then if it finally looked as if he still might lose whatever contest was in progress, well, he'd suddenly become the most noble, trustworthy guy in the world. He'd say *please* with his pale eyes all misty and sad and expect you to give in to him, just because he was so damn *sincere.*

For the first time since Darrell had appeared at the door, Slow spoke without thinking first. "You gave it your best shot, college boy. But you still didn't manage to slide that ring on her finger. As far as I'm concerned, she's fair game.''

Darrell yanked his nose out of the air, leaving nobility behind in favor of dawning outrage. "What, exactly, are you implying?''

"That there's a side of her that you and her old man always liked to pretend didn't exist, a side I wouldn't mind seeing just one more time..."

The other man sucked in air like a landed fish. "Why you— Are you saying you'll try to seduce her again? Is that what you're telling me?''

"Figure it out for yourself, Darrell."

"Why you—you are the most despicable, worthless piece of garbage either Violet or I have ever had the misfortune to know. As far as I'm concerned, there is nothing in this world too low for you to attempt. Nothing—I repeat—*nothing* is beneath you..."

Darrell ranted on, and Slow didn't interrupt him. By then the dangerous, hot recklessness that had claimed him briefly was cooling, leaving nothing but bitter disgust in its wake. And disgust not only at Darrell Carruthers but at himself, as well.

When he'd conceived the idea for his revenge, it had been a totally private thing, an old score he wanted to settle with Red alone. Even hinting at his plans to his old rival made it seem more like a sick contest between Darrell and him, with Violet little more than the prize in a game.

I'm as bad as he is, Slow thought, the bitter taste in his mouth growing stronger. And, just like him, I can't keep my damn mouth shut...

Slow stood, swiftly enough that Darrell started and fell back a step. "Forget it," Slow said. "This conversation is going nowhere fast. Allow me to show you the door.''

Darrell blinked, and perceived that he was shortly going to be thrown out. He intoned defiantly, ''I most certainly will not forget it.''

Slow threw up his hands. ''Then tell her. Tell her I said I was out to get in her pants. Tell her whatever you damn well please. It's all the same to me. But this discussion is terminated. You and I have got nothing more to say to each other.'' He herded the other man toward the front door. Darrell, nervous about what bad Slow Larkin might do if seriously provoked, allowed himself to be driven back.

At the door, Darrell drew himself up just as Slow reached for the knob. ''I have one more thing I'd like to say before I leave.''

''I'm listening.''

Darrell pursed his mouth, drew in a breath and said, ''I didn't set you up with the Corvette. And I never told Clovis Windemere that you were...seeing Violet.''

Slow waited a moment after Darrell spoke. Then he said, ''Your upper lip's sweating, Darrell.''

''I am telling you that I never—''

Slow waved his hand, as if batting away an irritating insect. ''Give me a break. I knew from your eyes the minute I threw all that old stuff out there that you did it—both times. And that's all I was after, really. To see your eyes when I asked you. What you *say* doesn't mean a damn thing to me.''

Darrell stuck his nose in the air again. ''Believe what you want, then.''

''I will.''

"And if you think you might convince Violet that I . . . did those things you mentioned, well, I am simply telling you that I'll deny it, as I'm denying it now."

"Darrell, don't lose any sleep over it, okay? It's the old Mexican standoff that we've got here. Neither of us is going to look too damn great if we talk. So you'll keep your mouth shut about what was said here today—and I'll do the same."

Chapter Eight

"What in the hell have you done to my front lawn?"

It was six-thirty at night. Violet stood in her stocking feet on the front porch, between the double columns. She clutched an iced tea in one hand and her high heels in the other and stared, appalled, out at the lawn, which appeared to have been savaged by some virulent species of rodent—perhaps a giant gopher, or a crazed mole.

She hadn't seen the damage right away, since the woodshed-garage was behind the house and she never passed the front of her house either going to or coming from work. A few minutes ago, she'd innocently entered the house through the kitchen, blissfully unaware that in her absence, Slow Larkin had decided to destroy her front yard.

She'd poured herself a cool iced tea and wandered out to the living room carrying her shoes in her free hand. Then she'd glanced out the window and witnessed the infuriating miscreant who haunted her dreams, shirtless as usual, hunched over a pothole in a crisscrossed series of ragged trenches in the middle of her mutilated lawn. She'd shot out the front door so fast her hair was still whipping in the wind she'd created.

Violet waved her shoes threateningly. "Slow. I asked you a question."

Slow looked up, flashed her some teeth and wiped the sweat from his brow with the back of his hand. "You could use a sprinkler system. I'm giving you one."

Violet began counting, very precisely, in her head, from one to ten. When she felt she could speak without screaming, she inquired, "Where is Lacy Jay?"

"Still at Glory's. She decided to stay for dinner."

"That's wonderful," Violet said.

"Yeah, those two really get along."

Actually Violet wasn't thinking so much of what great friends her mother and his daughter had become. More, she was thankful that a young child would not have to be witness to the things she planned to say the minute she got him inside where she could yell at him without restraint.

"Come inside," Violet said. "Now."

"Red." He tossed the wrench he was holding in the tool kit beside him and raised his arms to his sides. He looked down at his sweaty, mud-spattered, leanly muscled torso. "I'd love to. But I'm covered with dirt. And I'd like to get the front yard finished up before dark."

"The *front* yard," she repeated softly.

"Yeah, I'll do the back tomorrow. You're gonna love it. You set the timer and forget it. No more dragging that hose from one section to another."

"I'm going to love it."

"That's what I said."

"Please come inside. Now."

He shrugged and stood. "Tell you what. You get me a beer and I'll meet you on the back porch."

"Fine." She whirled and went back inside, trotting straight to her bedroom, where she dropped her shoes and slipped on a pair of soft moccasins, then stalked to the kitchen, yanked open the refrigerator door and grabbed the beer he wanted.

He was kneeling by the wooden swing that hung from the porch eaves when she shoved through the back screen. He looked up. "Get me that crescent wrench you keep in the kitchen drawer, will you?"

"What for?"

"This bolt is loose. It's dangerous. I'll tighten it."

"Forget the bolt. I have a few things to say to you." She approached him where he knelt on the other end of the swing. "Here's your beer." She held it out, keeping her body well away from him.

"Thanks." He drank and then set the can beside him. "Be right back." He was already on his feet again.

"Wait," she demanded as he laid a hand on the side of the porch railing and she realized he was about to leap over it.

He paused. "Yeah?"

"Where are you going?" She intended to sound commanding and instead sounded bewildered.

"To get a wrench from my tool kit, since you won't bring me the one inside."

"I said to forget that."

"I will. Just as soon as I fix it." He turned again.

She feared if he left, he might get reabsorbed in destroying her lawn and she'd never get him to stop. "Wait. I'll get the wrench."

He dropped to the railing instead of leaping it, then bent down and picked up his beer. "Thanks."

Grimly Violet returned to the kitchen, found the wrench and returned with it. She handed it over the same way as she had the beer, keeping the full length of her arm between them.

She took a tight sip from her iced tea and set it on the railing by the steps. She waited, fuming, as he tightened the bolt on the swing.

"There," he said after a minute. "That ought to do it." He stood and held the wrench toward her. She reached out quickly, before he could get too close, and took it from him. As the tool changed hands, she had a moment's absurd vision of how they must look—like two people passing something over an abyss.

She straightened, swiftly, and set the wrench by her tea glass.

Slow sat on the swing, which was suspended on chains from above. The joists overhead into which the chains were anchored creaked as they took his weight. Then he started the swing gently swaying. The suspending chains added more creaking as the links rubbed together. But the complaining of the old swing was a pleasant sound, actually—a reassuring sound. In all of Violet's memory, that swing had been on this porch. And it had always creaked and moaned whenever anyone sat in it.

"I always loved this old swing," Slow said.

Violet looked away, sharply, out over the yard to the fish pond near the back fence. When they were children, he had pushed her off that swing once because she'd told him he couldn't color in her coloring book until he washed his dirty hands. And then, of course, that swing was where they had shared their first incredible kiss, the one that had started everything way back when.

That night, in the starlit darkness, away from the dim yellow bulb that made a glow near the back door, they'd sat down on the swing, clutching hands, neither looking at each other.

Violet remembered now, with a funny tightness in her throat, how very carefully each of them had sat down, so that the swing wouldn't make a sound. It had seemed then, to Violet, as if they were under the sweet magic of a spell. And spells, after all, were tricky things. Anything might break them, and creaking sounds surely would.

They'd just sat there for a long time, not daring to swing, not looking at each other, saying nothing. Crickets chirped. Somewhere over toward Main Street a woman called a boy's name.

Then, out on the moon-silvered grass, Violet had seen what she'd assumed was a rock suddenly jump in the air, revealing a white belly that gleamed in the dark. Then the thing subsided to the grass and looked like a rock once more.

"Oh, look, Slow. A toad." She'd pointed with the hand that wasn't tightly holding his, and the swing had given a little creak or two when she moved.

He had laughed, low in his throat. And she had dared to look at him. His deep-set eyes looked black in the darkness. Black and soft and full of longings just like her own.

"Ever kiss a toad?" he asked.

That made her smile. "No."

"You got to watch out when you kiss a toad."

"You do?"

"Yeah. And never close your eyes."

"Why not?"

"Because when you open them . . ."

"What?"

"You might find out . . ."

"Yes?"

"That you've got warts on your lips."

Violet had stared at him, and then she'd started to laugh. He'd quickly put the pads of two fingers on her lips. "Shh . . . Want to try it?"

"What?" She felt her own breath, warm and seeking, as it flowed around his two fingers. Never in her young life had she been so totally aware of her own lips, of the softness of them against the slightly rougher skin of his finger pads.

"Kissing me," he said. His fingers drifted up her cheek, and then she realized that his other hand was on her face, too. He had slid her glasses off, leaving her feeling oddly naked—though since she was nearsighted, she could see him almost as well as before. It was everything else *but* him that went blurry and indistinct. He fumbled for her hand, and she felt the way his own hands shook. And he opened her fingers, slowly, as if they were the petals of some delicate flower that he feared he might bruise. He set her glasses in her palm.

She thought, as he was doing that, that she ought to tell him she didn't think he was a toad, not really.

She'd never thought of him as a toad. Honest. She thought of him as...scary, that was it. Scary in a tempting way. As if he burned with some kind of cruel, harsh brightness, casting dangerous, revealing light on her otherwise safe, unquestioned world.

She had told him, "Yes, I want to kiss you, Slow."

And she had, forgetting all about the creaking of the swing, the sound of which must have been what alerted her father to what was happening on the back porch. In a way, the noise of the old swing *had* broken the spell, after all.

"Hey," Slow said in a low voice now, summoning her back from that long-ago night.

Violet turned to him, still half-lost in the old memory.

He smiled at her, a soft smile. And for a moment she actually thought he would say something to indicate that he knew what she'd been remembering. She waited, half expecting to hear him tease, *Ever kiss a toad?*

But then he only said, "Talk to me," in a voice that assumed she had something very definite to say.

She almost asked him what he thought she should be talking about, and then remembered her mangled lawn. She picked up her tea and drained the last bit of it, mostly to give herself a few seconds to reorient her thoughts to the subject at hand.

She discovered something as she set the glass back down. Her anger had faded, somehow, while she remembered those enchanted moments on this very porch all those years ago. She was glad. It would make it easier to get to the bottom of what Slow Larkin was up to now.

She decided those very words would do for a start, so she asked them. "What are you up to now?"

He went on swinging the swing. "You mean with the sprinkler system?" he asked. Violet found herself surprised he admitted to knowing what she was talking about, rather than leaping up and announcing that he couldn't deal with her questions until he'd reshingled the roof or painted the garage door.

"The sprinkler system is exactly what I mean," she said.

He crushed his now empty beer can in his hands. "Are you worried I'll make a mess of it? Don't be. I know what I'm doing."

"I realize that," she conceded as she watched him idly turn the flattened cylinder he'd made of the can over and over in his hands. "You've always been good at—" she sought the words, "—mechanical things."

"Yeah. Good with my hands." He looked up at her, a look that was almost defiant.

"Yes," she agreed, thinking that his dexterity had never gotten him a lot of points with the father he'd hated, who'd wanted his only son to work with his brains, not his hands.

"Look sharp, Red," he said suddenly, flashing her a grin. He tossed the crushed can at her. She caught it, somewhat awkwardly, and set it by the wrench and her glass with the melting ice cubes in it.

"But the point is not that you'll do a good job," she went on. "The point is that you just did it, without so much as a word to me." She considered for a moment. "Or did you talk to my mother? Is that it?"

"Nope."

"Then I'll ask you again. Why?"

He grunted. "It's a way to pay you back, I guess. For having us here—whether you want us or not."

"But what about finding that garage space—and looking for a house to live in?"

The swing, which he'd been steadily rocking, stopped. The silence, minus the comfortable, steady creaking, had an ominous note to it. "I'll be out within a month, Red," he told her evenly. "I said I would. And *I* always keep my word."

Violet stiffened. "What are you saying, that *I* don't?" The minute the question was out, she longed to call it back. Eleven years ago she *hadn't* kept her word. If he pointed that out now, she herself would be substantially to blame for bringing up the old betrayal that was better left alone.

But Slow only looked at her steadily for a moment, and then began his unhurried rocking once more. The comfortable creaking recommenced, and Violet realized he was not going to rattle any more old skeletons right then.

Slow said, "Look. I would have told you about the sprinklers. But then you would have just said no."

"And that's my right. To say no."

"Yeah. But it wouldn't even have been open for discussion."

"That's my right, too. This is my house." She saw the look in his eyes and added, before he could, "Correction. My mother's house."

Slow looked at her for a moment, smugly, she thought. Then he grimaced a little, as if one of his gorgeous muscles had gotten a cramp. The next minute he was leaning way back in the swing, putting his hands behind his neck and straining his elbows out to the sides. He let out a low, luxurious groan when whatever had been paining him either stretched out or popped back into place.

Violet bit her lower lip, watching, intensely aware all over again of the pure physicality of him. Something in her solar plexus warmed, and she was suddenly feeling her own body, which was a little tired from sitting too much all day. There was a slight ache in her lower back, and her arches were sore from her high-heeled shoes.

Slow lowered his arms and their eyes met. "Nothing like digging a few trenches to make you know you're alive," he said.

"I'm sure," Violet said vaguely as she watched a little bead of sweat trickle down his jaw, slide along the side of his neck and then over his collarbone. When the small bead of moisture reached the T-shaped matting of hair on his chest, it got hung up and glinted there, right above his left nipple.

"Look," he said abruptly. "Do you want me to just rip out the pipes I laid and refill the trenches?"

Violet swallowed, thinking that the bead of sweat was so tiny she could have rid him of it using just the very tip of her tongue. "Refill the trenches?"

"That's what I said."

Violet blinked. This whole conversation, all of it, up to and including her earlier fury when she'd found out what he was doing, now seemed patently self-defeating.

She realized she was going to have to stop reacting before she thought things through. If she'd given the situation a minimum of consideration before leaping to the attack, then she wouldn't be standing here now, weak in the knees and moist between the legs, longing to lick the sweat off Slow Larkin's chest, when she ought to be in her kitchen thinking about what to stick in the microwave for dinner.

"Oh, what's the point?" she asked tiredly. "You'd only find some other way to drive me out of my mind. You might as well make yourself useful, I suppose. Just—do you think you could manage to warn me from now on, at least? So if I come home and find you've painted the place purple and put in a hot tub, I'll be a little bit prepared?"

He chuckled. "That's an idea. A hot tub..."

"Don't," she said flatly. "Just don't even think of it. Please."

He stood, and either didn't notice or pretended he didn't when she immediately fell back a step. "All right. No hot tub. And I promise, I'll warn you of any further improvements *before* I make them."

"Thank you."

He turned, and she realized he planned to leap the railing and return to his trenches. She stared at the marvelous symmetry of his back and the tight perfection of his buttocks. But then he was facing her again. "Oh, I almost forgot," he said.

"Yes?" The single word held more wariness than she once would have thought a mere syllable could possibly possess.

"Today I met the Ferrises next door and Mrs. Blaylock across Cottage Street. You know the Blaylocks have a boy about Lacy's age?"

"Yes, I know that." She waited. He was up to something. She could tell by how perfectly innocent he sounded.

"And the Ferrises have three little girls, ages two, six and ten."

"I know my own neighbors, Slow," Violet said with what she felt was an infinitely weary patience.

"No," Slow told her. "No, you don't. Not really. You know *of* them, and you're polite to them. But you don't really know them, not like people in a small town *should* know their neighbors."

"Just what are you getting at?" Violet asked in a quiet voice.

"Well, I just liked them a lot, that's all," he said.

"And?"

"And so I asked them all over for dinner, tomorrow. They were thrilled. I'm making spaghetti. We dig in at six."

Chapter Nine

"Umm. Yumm," said little Gretchen Ferris, aged two. Then she smashed a handful of spaghetti noodles, dripping red sauce, into her hair. The pasta slowly slithered down her fat cheek, leaving a red trail of sauce, and then plopped onto the arm of the ancient wooden high chair that Violet had brought down from the attic.

"Disgusting," muttered her big sister, Janine, across the table.

Slow, grinning from the head of the table, asked Bob Ferris if he'd like a little more wine. Bob eagerly agreed and filled his glass to the brim when Slow passed the bottle to him.

Violet, at the hostess's end of the table, gave Darrell, who sat silently to her right, a reassuring smile. It took him a minute to smile back, though he was looking straight at her. And then when he did smile, he did it nervously, glancing away and then back again.

Darrell was behaving very oddly, Violet thought. Of course, under the circumstances, he might be expected to be a little moody—but it was more than that. He seemed preoccupied and jumpy.

This morning when she'd casually mentioned that her neighbors were coming over for spaghetti, he'd asked if he was included. She'd said of course, thinking that Darrell and Slow, for the next month at least, were going to have to learn to get along. This dinner was as good a place to start as any.

She'd been nervous about it all day, though. Worried that the tension between the two men might flare into open hostility during the evening. She needn't have worried. The two seemed to have come to some kind of unspoken truce and were basically ignoring each other.

Slow was busy playing the role of host to the hilt. And Darrell was being . . . strange.

Perhaps, Violet thought, Darrell just wasn't accustomed to all the noise and confusion of having so many kids around. Maybe he found it a little overwhelming.

As if to punctuate Violet's thoughts, from halfway down the table little Gretchen suddenly crowed in delight. "Ooogy, noodles!" She smashed a wad of pasta against her mouth for a moment—and then threw what didn't fit inside across the table.

"Argh, gross!" exclaimed Evan Blaylock, Jr., nine, as some of the sauce hit his chin and several limp noodles sailed on past to splatter on the rug that Violet's grandmother had brought from Philadelphia along with the tea cart in the corner.

"Mother, Gretchen should be punished for that," insisted Janine Ferris. Janine was ten and appeared to consider it her duty to see that retribution was meted out immediately when any other child misbehaved. She was also a perfect little lady, in a powder blue dress and matching flats. Earlier she'd asked Lacy Jay if it bothered her that she looked just like a boy.

"More wine, Darrell?" Bob Ferris asked, holding up the bottle.

"Thank you," Darrell said stiffly. "I believe I will."

Violet grinned to herself, thinking that she wasn't used to having all these kids around, either—but that she could *get* used to it. It was kind of fun wondering which kid would do what next.

Violet forked up another meatball and put her concern about Darrell aside. Things were bound to be a little strained, given the situation. And she had enough troubles without going out looking for them.

The rambunctious dinner continued.

Down at the other end of the table, next to Slow, Glorianna was expounding about her life in the theater, apparently in response to something six-year-old Callie Ferris had whispered in her ear. Callie, Violet had learned, was going through a shy stage and only communicated by whispering in people's ears.

Violet turned to Martha Blaylock on her left as the other woman inquired about garden pests. Violet answered that she herself was having no problem with spider mites on the roses this year. Martha was just asking her about alternatives to malathion dust as an insecticide when quiet little Callie suddenly let out a piercing wail and leaped from her seat into Glorianna's lap, knocking her plate to the floor in the process.

Violet excused herself from the conversation with Martha, rose quickly to find a roll of paper towels and joined Reba Ferris in scraping spaghetti and Italian dressing off the rug. But then Callie cried, "Mama!" and Reba took the child from Glorianna.

"Oh, I'm so sorry," Reba moaned as she rocked her child, while Violet stayed on the floor to rake up the food. "This is awful. Tomato sauce and oil. I could just die."

"It'll clean," Violet said, glancing up and giving the other woman a smile.

"Oh, Lord, I hope so." Reba groaned, and then crooned to Callie, "Now settle down, honey. It's all right. It's fine. Tell Mommy what happened."

Glorianna volunteered, "She whispered to me that Evan, Jr. pinched her."

"Oh, gross," Evan, Jr. said. "I didn't!"

"Evan, Jr." Evan, Sr. intoned his son's name in a voice that spoke of dire consequences to little boys who didn't tell the truth.

Beneath the freckles across his nose, Evan, Jr. flushed. "Well, she keeps *whispering*. It bugs me. I hate *whispering*. Can't she talk like normal people?"

"It's not right to pinch," Janine Ferris interjected in righteous tones. "Pinching *hurts*. Evan, Jr. should be punished."

"And you should mind your own business," Lacy Jay advised.

"Lacy," Slow warned.

Lacy Jay looked at her father, and then slumped in her chair and folded her arms across her chest.

Janine Ferris flushed in triumph. "As I was saying, Evan, Jr. needs to learn a lesson."

"That's enough, Janine," Bob Ferris said.

"Evan," the boy's father said. "Apologize to Callie and tell her you won't do that again."

Evan pursed his lips and stared at his lap.

"Make him stay in his room for a *year*," Janine gleefully suggested.

"One more word from you, young lady..." Janine's father advised.

Janine blinked and stuck her lip out, but said no more.

"Apologize," Evan, Sr. demanded again.

"All right," Evan, Jr. gave in at last. "I 'pologize. I won't do it again."

Callie Ferris sniffed bravely, narrowed her huge blue eyes at Evan as if gauging his sincerity and then whispered in her mother's ear.

"Callie say it's all right," Reba Ferris solemnly told Evan, Jr.

Violet rose with the remains of Callie's meal in one hand and her trusty roll of paper towels in the other as Reba Ferris settled little Callie back in her chair and promised to get her another plate of food.

Violet and Reba were just turning to head, side by side, for the kitchen when there was a click and a crash from across the table. The two women turned in tandem.

"Oh, yuck!" Lacy exclaimed, bouncing out of her chair as half of baby Gretchen's overturned milk splattered her jeans before dribbling on down to the rug.

"Oh, yuck!" baby Gretchen agreed, peering over the tray of the old high chair to the rug below where her milk and her dinner had landed. "Make a mess!" the baby shouted with relish.

"Lord, Lord." Reba sighed.

"Go on and get Callie's food—and more for Gretchen, too, I think." Violet handed the other woman the dirty plate. "I'll take care of the mess."

With a grateful smile, Reba disappeared into the butler's pantry. Violet headed for the other side of the long table, but was stopped by a hand on her arm before she got there.

Slow grinned at her. "My turn." He held out his other hand. For a moment, in spite of the eleven other people in the room, all she could think of was the tantalizing little shiver his touch brought.

Then Slow stood and she passed him the roll of towels. He released her. Absurdly she felt the loss of his touch as much as the touch itself. He moved around the table and knelt beside Gretchen's high chair.

"Dad, I gotta go change," Lacy said as Slow patiently mopped up the milk and noodles.

Slow rolled off a few towels and handed them to his daughter. "Try these first."

"Messy, messy!" Gretchen crowed. "Make a messy! Yeah, yeah!"

"Gretchen needs a lesson . . ." Janine muttered under her breath.

Bob Ferris shot his oldest daughter a level warning stare and then slid off his chair to crouch beside Slow and chase down a few recalcitrant noodles that had slithered under the table.

"Well," Lacy said. "I guess my jeans will be okay, after all."

Slow looked up long enough to give his daughter a grin.

At that point, Violet realized she'd been standing there beside Slow's empty chair, staring musingly after him, since he released her arm. She ordered her legs to move and started for her own end of the table. When she got there, she sat down quickly and was careful not to look at Darrell, who sat, very quietly, beside her.

The dinner continued, more of the same, for half an hour longer. Then they all filed out to the back porch for watermelon.

There, Lacy and Evan, Jr. engaged in a seed-spitting contest while Janine groused that people who spit seeds were rude and probably should at *least* be benched for an hour or so. Lacy bore that criticism for a while without exacting retribution. But then she began aiming her seeds in Janine's direction. Janine began yelping and then both of them were benched to either end of the porch swing.

In the meantime, Gretchen toddled off the porch and gnawed on some green walnuts from the foot of the tree by the garage, while Callie sat on Glorianna's lap and whispered endless secrets in her ear.

Once the watermelon was gone, Violet, Reba Ferris and Glorianna's sweet-natured Arthur wandered inside to start on the dishes. But they'd barely straightened up the dining room when Slow came in and found them. He ordered them back outside where the action was, insisting that he would finish cleaning up later himself.

Outside, Slow had set up an ancient croquet game he'd found in the garage. He got everyone playing, except Darrell, who said he'd prefer to watch. Even plump little Gretchen dragged a mallet around, beating at the wooden balls with it and trying to unearth the hoops.

Slowly, over the surrounding hillsides, the pines turned black as the shadows claimed them. Darrell, so silent and restless all evening, was the first to say he had to leave. Violet walked him to his car.

They went through the house, not touching. When they reached his BMW, he took her hand.

"Thanks for coming," she said lamely, pulling her fingers free.

He stared at her with a mournful expression—like a beloved dog who has suddenly been told he has to sleep on the back porch from now on. Then he bravely forced a smile.

"All those kids," he said, clearly relieved to be away from them. "People like the Ferrises ought to try birth control."

"They only have three," she reminded him, feeling suddenly defensive for the children. "And I think they're great."

"They're undisciplined," Darrell said.

"Well, maybe they get a little out of hand sometimes, but—"

"*Sometimes?* Come now, Violet. They're practically savages."

"They're sweet girls."

"Sweet? *Sweet?* That baby eats like an animal, and the middle one has some psychological problem, with all that whispering. And the oldest, well, when I was a child I would never have been allowed to say *half* the things she says. And that little girl of Slow's—she looks to me like a serious case of gender confusion, at the very least."

"That is enough," Violet said, her irritation turning to cold fury when he began to criticize Lacy Jay.

"Lacy Jay is a terrific kid, period. And if you think otherwise, just keep it to yourself."

Darrell blinked. "Violet? What's gotten into you? I was only—"

Telling me how you *really* feel about children, she thought. But what she said aloud was, "Look, let's drop it. It's a subject on which we simply don't agree."

He blinked again, then rushed to concur with her. "Yes. Of course. You're absolutely right."

"And I should get back." She stepped aside and opened his car door for him.

"Certainly." He slid behind the wheel. "I'll—I'll see you tomorrow. I'm in court at nine. But maybe I'll give you a buzz when we break and we could meet at Cirino's for lunch?"

"That would be nice. Good night, Darrell."

He started up the car and pulled out. She waved to him, briefly. Then she went in the gate and headed for the back by going around the house. She heard the laughter and exclamations of the others as soon as she reached the side of the house, and she grinned, eager to rejoin the fun.

She was parallel with her own bedroom when she spotted little Gretchen on her fat knees under the snowball bush at the corner of the house.

"Gretchen?" Violet asked.

The toddler pulled her head out of the bush, pushed herself to her feet and burst into a huge, toothy grin. "Bi-let!" she exclaimed, as if Violet were a very old friend whom she hadn't seen in years. Then, arms out, she toddled over. "Hold you!" she commanded, when she stood in front of Violet.

Violet reached down to lift the child and found herself engulfed in the mingled smells of garden dirt and tomato sauce and talcum powder, along with that lovely scent that only babies have, a fragrance like fresh-baked bread.

"Kiss?" Gretchen inquired when she was up in Violet's arms.

"Yes," Violet answered. "Yes, kiss."

Very intently, Gretchen sucked in the sides of her lips, until she looked like a stunned fish. Then she placed her own baby version of a pucker on Violet's cheek and made a loud smacking noise.

"There. Kiss," she announced proudly when she was done.

"Thank you," Violet said, deriving boundless pleasure from the feel of the plump weight against her breasts and the fat arms around her neck. She nuzzled the baby, ruffling her downy strawberry-colored hair, thinking that babies like this were what life was all about—babies that grew into little girls who became young women who in turn had babies of their own.

In her arms, Gretchen began to squirm. "Down, Bilet. Now."

Violet chuckled against her pink cheek, stole one more tiny kiss and set her down. "There," she said. "Is that what you wanted?"

"Looks about right," said a voice from over by the snowball bush.

The familiar shiver prickled her skin and Violet stood, releasing the baby, to peer through the encroaching twilight into Slow's eyes.

Gretchen grunted and toddled back toward the main part of the yard, but Violet was hardly aware of her anymore. She only saw Slow. And she felt—what? Revealed, perhaps.

She wondered how long he had watched her with the baby, and then she wondered why it should matter how long he'd been standing there. Except that during the brief week of love they'd once shared, she'd told him she wanted a huge house with lots of kids in it, and he had laughed and agreed that that was just fine with him.

"We've got a minor disaster," he said after a moment where neither spoke and the excited babble in the yard swelled to fill the heavy silence between the two of them.

"Yes?" Her voice sounded faraway, lost in a memory of things they'd said long ago. She forced herself to speak more firmly. "What is it?"

He chuckled. "Just as you went into the house, Callie knocked a ball into the fish pond."

"Well, that's no problem. I'll just get the big fishnet and we can troll for it."

"Too late for that," he told her. "Evan, Jr. jumped in to rescue it."

"Is he all right?"

"He's fine. But the Blaylocks have decided to get him on home and into some dry duds." He signaled with a jerk of his head. "Come on. They're looking for you to tell you what a great time they had." He turned, and Violet followed him around the corner to the back porch where everybody had gathered around Evan, Jr., who was still dripping a little and wrapped in a towel from the downstairs bathroom.

"There you are!" Martha Blaylock said when Violet appeared in their midst. "We hate to go, but we must. It was wonderful, such great fun."

The whole group flooded into the house and through the pantry to the main hall. Martha hugged

Violet briefly before they went out the door. "We'll do it again soon," she suggested, turning to peel the towel from around her son's shoulders and then handing it to Lacy Jay. "How about at our house next time?"

Everyone agreed that was a great idea and they all stood on the front porch and waved as the Blaylocks crossed the street to their own house on the opposite corner. Then Reba Ferris decided that it was past Gretchen's bedtime and they should be on their way, too.

"Bye-bye. Come 'gain soon." Gretchen waved her fat fist as Callie whispered her thanks to Slow, and Janine pointed out that Evan, Jr. really hadn't received a punishment for jumping in the fish pond.

"Thanks," Reba Ferris said, her usually harried face lightened by a smile. "If you think you can take it, we'll try my house after Martha's turn."

"Sounds great," Slow said as he shook Bob's hand.

Violet tensed a little, wondering what he'd told her neighbors about their living situation. They all seemed to assume that he'd be around for a long time to come. Slow glanced briefly at Violet and then added, with barely a pause, "Even if Lacy and I have found our own place by then, we'd love to come."

Violet relaxed, and found herself smiling at him for making it clear to her neighbors that he was just a temporary guest. He smiled back. And she couldn't help thinking again, as Glorianna and Arthur departed, that the evening had been really *fun*.

And, unbelievably, she found herself telling him as much a few minutes later when the three of them— Slow, Lacy Jay and herself—had returned to the kitchen to load up the dishwasher and scrub out the pots.

He said, "Yeah. It's the kind of thing you've always liked."

Poised over the dishwasher with a handful of flatware in her fist, she glanced up at him. She was thinking that he *did* remember what she'd said once about that big, noisy house with all the kids in it. What else in her quiet, single life would lead him to suspect that what she really longed for was spaghetti on the carpet and croquet balls in the goldfish pond?

She almost whispered, You *do* remember. . . .

But stopped herself before the words took form.

"Can I go watch TV now?" Lacy Jay asked. "I dried the pots and the salad bowl and the rest goes in the dishwasher."

"Okay, get lost," Slow told her and took the towel from her outstretched hand. She left the room like a streak before Slow or Violet could find something else for her to dry. A minute later, from the living room, they heard the drone of the television.

For a while after that they worked without speaking, Violet loading the dishwasher, Slow wiping down counters. In the window over the sink, and the one along the outside wall, Violet could see flashes of their reflections, working smoothly as if they'd been cleaning up after guests together for years.

"I'm going to get the back sprinklers in tomorrow," he said then. "I put it off today because I figured if I didn't get the grass back down, we couldn't turn the kids loose back there after dinner."

"That was smart," Violet heard herself remarking, and thought that anyone glancing in those windows might think they saw a married couple, doing the dishes, talking over plans for the next day. . .

"And did you know Evan's a real-estate agent?" he was asking.

"Yes. Yes, I think I remember him telling me that."

"He thinks he has a few possibilities for the garage space I need. And he's also going to work with me on finding the right house."

"That's great." Violet slid the last plate in place on the rack and realized that her thoughts had turned to Lacy Jay, to what a good father Slow was. She found herself wondering about what Lacy was like at Gretchen's age—and about Lacy's mother, Loni, the stunt driver who had been Slow's wife. "Slow?"

"Yeah?" He was hanging the dish towel on the rack, and he paused, turning to look over his shoulder at her.

Violet closed the dishwasher and leaned against it, bracing her hands behind her on the lip of the counter. "It's none of my business, I know..."

"What?"

"But I've always kind of wondered..." She couldn't believe she was doing this. But somehow, after tonight, she didn't feel quite so threatened by him.

And apart from a few salacious remarks, he hadn't actually *done* anything to make her think she needed to fear him. If she'd thought at first that he might be out to prove to her that she couldn't resist him if he felt like seducing her, she wasn't so sure about that now. In the three days that he'd been here, he'd never once even tried to kiss her.

Whatever he was up to, she was gradually beginning to believe it had little to do with sex. Truthfully it was more her own forbidden desires taunting her than anything he'd done that sometimes drove her crazy. She was beginning to believe, as much as it hurt her pride to admit it, that Slow Larkin had little, if any, interest in getting into her bed.

And she *had* always wondered about what Loni McDermott was like, and about what the other woman and Slow had shared.

When Violet had heard of their marriage, she'd wanted to die for a while—though she'd locked that wish down deep in her most secret heart. She'd known she had no right to such self-indulgence because, after all, she herself had sent him away.

"You wondered what?" Slow prompted.

"About Loni..." There, she'd done it. Said the name, forced it out right around the stone that seemed to be lodged in her throat.

She waited, her stomach tightening in anxiety, for him to growl at her that she was right—it *was* none of her business.

But he completely surprised her by smiling. "Yeah? What did you want to know?"

She coughed, in mingled relief and excitement. All these years, wondering about the woman Slow Larkin had married. And finding out about her was as simple as asking.

"How did you meet her?"

"I built a car for her, one she needed for a special stunt. A '58 Plymouth Fury with a breakaway body, so by the end of the stunt she'd be driving on just the frame and the wheels." He chuckled. "She asked me out—Loni generally went right after anything she wanted."

"So you dated, and then after a while you decided you loved her and wanted to marry her?"

"Well, not exactly," he said. He paused then to go to the refrigerator for a beer, tossing her one, too, when she nodded in response to his questioning look. They sat down opposite each other at the breakfast table by the side window. "I wasn't…going out much at the time," he said. "I told her I was trying to start a new business and didn't have a lot of time for women. But Loni was relentless. Maybe I was like a new stunt to her. She went at me like that—with unswerving determination and flawless attention to detail.

"She sent me singing telegrams and model cars with invitations to lunch inside. And I started to *like* her, you know? She was so driven and passionate about her work, and she knew where she was going. And she told me she was looking for a man who was exactly the same way. We became lovers, and then one day she came to me and said that she'd messed up and was pregnant. And if I was willing to marry her and take at least fifty percent of the responsibility for the kid, she would keep it. So I did—and she did."

Violet drank from her beer. "You make it sound a little like a business agreement."

He stared at his own reflection in the window, his thoughts faraway. "Maybe it was, in a way. But we were pretty good together. We got along. We were true to each other. And it worked out. I guess, really, we wanted the same things from each other. A partner in raising Lacy Jay, a friend. We made an agreement, and we both stuck to it, until she died. She wasn't the love of my life and I wasn't hers. *Risk* was Loni's great love." He took a drink from his beer, and then set the can on the table and stared at it. "And eventually she took one risk too many. She was a terrific lady. And I miss her." He glanced up to catch Violet's eye. "Is that what you wanted to know?"

"Yes," she answered, ignoring the selfish question that echoed in her head: Who *was* the love of your life, if not Loni? Was it me, Slow? Was it me? "Thank you. For telling me," she said softly.

"Anytime." He went on looking at her, a funny, unreadable expression on his face. Then he cleared his throat. "Well." He looked around. "Things look taken care of in here."

"Yes. Taken care of."

"You gonna turn that thing on?" He gestured with his beer toward the dishwasher.

"Oh." She quickly stood. "Right."

He stood, too. "Think I'll just wander on in the living room and monitor my kid's television viewing. Gotta watch out for those exploding heads."

She gave a nervous little laugh. "Yes. Good idea." Then she turned and looked under the sink for the dishwasher detergent. She didn't hear him slip away, but when she turned back to the room, he wasn't in it.

Not really even thinking that she was following him, she trailed into the living room. He stood against the arch to the dining room, looking at Lacy Jay, who was fast asleep on the floor, the pages of *Blood City,* the horror story Lacy and Glorianna had written, open beneath her outflung arm.

Slow heard Violet's approaching step and turned his head to look at her. "She's a hopeless day person," he said softly, gazing down at Lacy once more.

Violet stared back at him, remembering how they once had laughed about that—a day person and a night person, how would they ever make it work?

She had the most dangerous urge then, to go to him, to put her hands on his shoulders, to demand, *How much do you remember about us, really? And what does it mean to you? What is it worth to you? Can't you please tell me now why you're here?*

But she couldn't quite do it. Not yet. Perhaps, the cowardly part of her hedged, not ever.

She forced her gaze back to the sleeping child and felt soothed. Lacy looked so tender, her mouth so soft. Her hair, slicked back so carefully this morning, lay in light brown swatches against her cheeks.

"Bedtime," Violet murmured.

Slow left the arch and knelt to gather his daughter against his chest. He rose and headed for the stairs.

Not even stopping to wonder if continuing to go where he went was wise, Violet gathered up the pages of *Blood City* and mounted the steps in his wake.

In the little corner room they helped Lacy out of her shoes and jeans and studded wristband. Then they tucked her beneath the covers still wearing her T-shirt as a nightgown. Slow kissed her, and Violet kissed her, and then they went to the open door together.

"It was a fun dinner," Lacy murmured from the bed as Slow switched off the lights. "It's not so bad here, after all, I guess. Except for Janine Ferris, I could probably get used to Nevada City."

"Night, Lacy," Slow said.

"Night, Dad."

Slow and Violet went back down the stairs together, neither speaking. Violet was thinking how strange it was, because it all seemed very natural—to tuck Lacy into bed and then wander back to the living room side by side.

Something was happening, something she never would have imagined. She was starting to *like* Slow, to feel comfortable around him. In a mere three days, it was starting to seem so normal to have him in her house, to sit across the table from him at dinner and to help tuck his child into bed come nighttime.

At the foot of the stairs she turned to him, thinking that maybe she might just tell him that. He smiled at her.

"What?" he asked.

But she went no further because the door chimes rang.

It was only a few steps to the door. She opened it. And found Darrell standing there.

Chapter Ten

In the yellow glare of the porch light, Darrell's face had a greenish cast. He looked strung tight with tension.

"Darrell? What—"

"It's my parents," he said. "They've been in an accident. In Idaho." He said the name of the state incredulously, as if accidents had never before been allowed to happen there.

"Oh, my God. Are they all right?"

"They're alive. But Dad's in surgery right now. And Mom's got a broken hip and both arms fractured. I can't get a flight that'll get me to Boise until tomorrow at the earliest, so I'm just going to go ahead and drive it."

"Of course."

"I was going to call you, but then I wanted to—" He glanced beyond her and saw Slow, still standing with one foot on the stair. He glared at Slow and then refocused on Violet once more. "I wanted to see you before I left." He lowered his voice. "May I have a minute? Alone."

"I was just on my way back upstairs anyway," Slow said, taking the hint without argument. He turned, and then seemed to decide there was one more thing he had to say. He turned back again. "It's a rough break, Darrell. But they're alive and that's what counts."

Darrell said nothing, only stared at Slow with a frozen glare. Slow shrugged and went on up the stairs. Darrell clasped Violet's hand. "Come outside with me. I need to get going, but there's something I have to say first."

She didn't protest as he pulled her out the door and down the steps. He stopped when they'd moved out of the revealing glare of the porch light and into the shadow of the linden tree.

"I don't know how long I'll have to be gone," Darrell said.

"Don't worry about things here," Violet reassured him. She was a little worried about him driving all night in such an emotionally overwrought state. She rushed to put his mind at ease about his calendar, at least. "Melinda can fill me in on everything." Melinda was his secretary. "I'll call her right now and ask her to come in at seven to go over your calendar. And then as soon as I've met with her, I'll get right over to the courthouse for the hearing at nine. It will all work out fine."

"But what about Thursday?" he reminded her darkly. "We have conflicting court dates. I've got the Lonigan personal injury suit, and you've got that Chapter Seven in Sacramento." There was a trace of disapproval in his tone. The Chapter Seven bankruptcy was one of Violet's *pro bono* cases—assumed without charge to the client. Darrell had never been thrilled about the cases Violet took on for free.

"Darrell, it will work out," she soothed. "I'll get a continuance on one of them if I have to."

"Which one?"

"Probably your Lonigan case. And don't look at me like that. If I've got to get a postponement on one of them, I'd rather it be the one I'm least prepared for."

"We are looking at a settlement of ten thousand, at least, for the Lonigan case."

Violet sighed. "Darrell, this couldn't be helped. The judge will understand. Now stop worrying. Things will be just fine here."

He managed a brave smile. "I suppose you're right."

"I know I am. You'll have plenty to do in Idaho. I'll manage fine here."

He looked at her for a moment, then said carefully, "I know you will when it comes to the firm.... But Violet..." He pulled her closer by her captured hand and then wrapped his arms around her. She allowed him that because she was concerned for him, though his arms, like his every touch lately, felt alien and wrong. She craned her head back, partly so she could see his face and partly to give herself a little distance from him.

"Yes, what is it, Darrell?"

"Violet, just...wait until I get back. Will you do that for me?"

"Wait?" she asked, suspecting what he meant but wishing she didn't.

"Don't...do anything foolish while I'm not here to look out for you, all right?"

Violet stiffened and squirmed free of his hold. She longed to tell him in no uncertain terms that she was a full-grown woman and hardly required looking after. But then she reminded herself that he was under enough stress as it was, and she didn't want him driving off into the night with a harsh reprimand from her ringing in his ears, as well.

She said in an extremely reasonable tone, "My actions are up to me, Darrell. Please respect that."

He combed his pale hair back with his fingers and then drew in a deep breath. "Violet. Please. We need to talk again. A long talk. Don't go rushing into anything with *him,* no matter what he tells you, until we've talked."

"What are you saying, Darrell? Is there something I don't know?"

"No—yes. Please just wait. Until I come back. Then I'll explain everything. And everything will be worked out."

"Explain *what?*"

He looked at her, his eyes full of frustration. And then he said, "Nothing. Never mind. There's nothing. I'm just frantic about my parents, that's all. And worried about leaving you alone with that creep in your house."

"I can take care of myself, Darrell. And nothing's going to happen between Slow and me." She said the words with complete assurance. If, secretly, she couldn't trust herself, she was becoming pretty certain that she *could* trust Slow. The ego-flaying truth was he didn't want her anyway, or he would have done something by now.

"Promise?" Darrell pleaded.

"Darrell, you're carrying this too far."

"Why?" Now his expression turned hard. "*Is* something going to happen—or has it already?"

"You are completely out of line!" Violet took a step back and turned away in order to get a better grip on her growing anger.

She could hardly believe the way he was acting. She and Darrell had an agreement. She had no commitment to him until at least after Slow had gone and everything could be reevaluated. Still here he was, behaving just like a jealous lover—demanding to know if she'd betrayed him with another man and begging her to remain true to him in his absence.

"Violet?" Darrell said from behind her.

"What?" She turned to face him once more and saw in the dim light that his expression had changed again. His accusing wrath had fled as if it had never been and he wore a pleading look once more.

"I'm sorry." He rushed to placate her. "You're right. That was a rotten thing to ask you. I take it back. Please forgive me. I'm—I'm distraught about my parents is all. And I don't want to drive all night worried about them *and* you. Can't you see that I'm just looking for a little reassurance? You can give that to me by indulging my silly jealousy and promising to do what I know you already intend to do—stay away from Slow."

Violet crossed her arms under her breasts, gripping both elbows, considering what Darrell had just said.

He was right about one thing, she decided. He *did* have to drive all night and she didn't want him any more upset than he already was. Besides that, he had another point: what possible harm could reassuring him do? She wouldn't be getting involved with Slow anyway, so why not go ahead and give Darrell the peace of mind he so desperately needed?

She decided to give in to his request—though deep down she knew it was not something he had the right to ask of her. "All right, then," she said. "Nothing's going to happen between Slow and me while you're gone. I promise you that."

Darrell's strained expression relaxed considerably. "Thank you, darling," he said with great dignity. He took her in his arms again and kissed her. She acquiesced to that, feeling stiff and uncomfortable as his lips brushed against hers.

He released her at last, and then they walked around the looming black form of Slow's car and across the street to where Darrell's car was parked. He got in. "I'll call you with a phone number and an address the minute I find out what's going on."

"Please drive carefully, Darrell."

He told her he would as he started up the car. Violet stood, watching, until his taillights disappeared down Broad Street. Then she walked back to the house, her arms still wrapped around herself as though to ward off a chill, though the August night was warm.

Slow was nowhere in sight when she let herself in the door. She went right to the phone in the dining room and called Darrell's secretary, who promised to meet her promptly at seven. When she hung up, she noticed that the TV in the living room still droned on. She went to it and switched it off.

She was standing there, staring sightlessly at the big easy chair where Slow always sat now, when she heard his voice from the hall.

"You okay?"

She started, since she hadn't heard him come down.
Then she noticed that he'd taken off his boots, which
explained his quiet approach. She stared at his stocking feet for a moment, made poignantly aware all over
again that he was a fixture in her house for a good time
to come. And he'd certainly made himself comfortable. He prowled her kitchen bare chested when he finally rose from bed at noon, and at night he stalked
her stairs without his boots.

"Red?" He asked her name, and she heard the
honest concern in his voice.

She recalled that he'd asked her if she was okay. She
answered, "I'm fine."

"I heard you come in and thought . . ." He paused,
as if he wasn't quite sure *what* had brought him back
downstairs. Then he shrugged. "I don't know. I just
wanted to see if you were all right."

"Well." She made her lips form a smile. "I am. All
right. Or at least as all right as can be expected."

"I'm sure they'll pull out of it fine."

"Darrell's parents?"

"Yeah."

She found herself thinking that she was rather glad
Slow had come down. Having him to talk to would
keep her from dwelling on certain distressing thoughts
that kept taunting her. Thoughts about the conversation she'd just had with Darrell. And about how Darrell's behavior seemed, in retrospect, like flagrant
emotional blackmail.

Thinking back over what had been said beneath the
linden tree, she couldn't help but feel that Darrell had
used her concern over his safety on the highway to get
her to promise to keep away from Slow.

In fact, lately it seemed that a lot of things to do with Darrell weren't right. As if the man she'd known all her life, with whom she'd grown up, were changing into someone she didn't know at all, someone overbearing and impatient. Someone who said he wanted a big family but hated being around children. Someone who would stop at nothing to get things his way.

Slow chuckled.

"What's so funny?" Violet asked, eager to share the joke and take her mind off the chilling thought that Darrell was actually someone she hardly knew.

"Nothing much," Slow said. "Just thinking."

"Of what?" she prompted.

"About our fathers—yours, mine and Darrell's. And that I always liked Darrell, Sr. the best."

Violet was intrigued. "Why?"

"Well, *your* old man always hated me. And you know how *my* father and I got along. But I kind of liked Darrell's dad, so quiet and absentminded." Slow grinned his devilish grin. "And then, of course, he had the good sense to own a Corvette...."

"Which got you into very hot water once," she said teasingly, not stopping to think that the subject might still be a sensitive one with him.

He tipped his head, as if gauging hidden meanings in what she'd said. And then he shrugged and left the archway to enter the room.

"I'm sorry," she hastened to tell him as he crossed the room and dropped into the big easy chair. "I probably shouldn't make light of it. That was a... difficult time for you."

He surprised her by what he said next. "It was the best thing that could have happened to me, really. It

was time to cut the cord between me and my father."
He hoisted his feet up on the ottoman. "The army
gave me a chance to start over. It worked out fine."

Something rose up in Violet then, a protectiveness
toward the man who sat across the room from her. She
said, "It was only a joyride that you took in that car.
They were way too rough on you."

"Technically it was grand theft."

"Sometimes the spirit of the law is better served by
tempering justice with mercy."

Slow laughed. "That's what you said eleven years
ago. Remember?"

She looked at him. Oh, how she remembered. When
they became lovers, she'd told him just how outraged
she'd been that they'd sent him off to the service for
borrowing Darrell, Sr.'s car. She'd also felt as if she
were a little to blame—since he was already in disgrace for what had happened between them out on the
back porch the night before. Darrell, Sr. and Slow's
father had put their heads together and come up with
the choice for punishment for Slow's stealing the
precious Corvette: Darrell, Sr. would go ahead and
press charges—or Slow could enlist.

"You were treated badly," Violet said again, thinking of the choice those two men had forced Slow to
make. "By all of us."

"Except your mother," he reminded her.

It was Violet's turn to chuckle. "Mother always
adored you. You're so...dramatic. Mother adores
anyone or anything dramatic." Then she became serious once more. "But Mother couldn't help you then.
They shipped you off to the service, and your father
disowned you—"

"Wait a minute." He put up a hand. "Maybe we ought to clear that part up."

"What do you mean?"

"I mean, the day my father died he told me he would call in Clovis and put me back in his will. But I told him not to."

"You what?" Violet stared at him, incredulous.

"I was young," he explained. "I had some stupid idea that his money was poison after how much we'd hated each other. So I told him to keep it, I'd make it on my own. He asked me then if I was sure that was what I wanted. I said yes. And he said, 'Fair enough.'" Slow made a disgusted sound in his throat. "I could have shot myself two days later when you came to my door to express your condolences and I invited you in and, well, you know what happened next. As soon as I realized I was in love with you, I saw what an idiot I'd been to turn down my father's money. I had nothing to offer you."

Violet stared at him, a funny warmth in her belly at his words. *I was in love with you,* he'd said. But of course that was in the past tense. Dead and buried. At least as far as he was concerned...

Slow continued. "And then later, when I had Lacy, I really could have kicked myself. That money should have been hers. But at the time the old man offered to give me back my inheritance, I wasn't thinking how something might happen between you and me, or that someday I'd have a kid. I was only thinking that I didn't want his tainted money."

"But you never told me that you made up with your father," Violet said, feeling slightly hurt that he hadn't trusted her to tell her, though she knew the feeling was misplaced—that had been a long time ago.

Slow grunted. "I wasn't about to let you know then that I was not only flat broke, but I was flat broke *on purpose.*"

Violet thought about that. Then she said, softly, "But in the end you did what you set out to do. You made it on your own. And Lacy will do just fine without money from a grandfather she never even knew."

"That's what I keep telling myself," Slow said.

"It was your dad's loss, really," Violet went on, meaning every word she said. "That he'll never get to know Lacy. That he never gave himself a chance to know you."

"You think so?"

"Yes, I do."

"I would do it all differently," he said. "Now that I'm older."

"But..." She had to swallow, suddenly finding more than the surface meaning in his words. "But we can't go back."

"No." He smiled at her, a shadowed smile that looked almost sad. "We can't go back."

"There's only now."

"Yes," he agreed. "Now." His eyes looked so deep, fathomless, as he smiled at her. She felt her own answering smile take shape, a slight lifting of the corners of her mouth, a tremulous thing.

"Slow?"

"Yeah?"

"Do you..." The words were so hard to find, but she struggled to pronounce them anyway. "I understand that you came back here to give Lacy a better place to grow up, but..."

"Yeah?"

"Is that the only reason?"

He said nothing for a moment. At last he answered, "No."

"I knew it," she said. "I knew there was more. I think I understand now—about the other reason you came back."

"You do?"

"Yes."

"Suppose *you* tell *me,* then."

"Well..." She felt embarrassed suddenly. "At first I thought, as I said the other night, that you wanted some kind of *revenge* on me for what happened eleven years ago. But I realize now that my assumption was all wrong—that I only thought that because of my own feelings of guilt."

"Because you dumped me, you mean?" He was looking at her a little strangely now, Violet thought. But then it was a difficult subject, and both of them were just trying to be honest, and that wasn't always easy, after all.

"Yes," she admitted with effort. "Because I sent you away."

"But now," he prompted, "you think it's something else I'm after—other than revenge?"

"Yes. I do. I think in your own way you want to put all the old resentments to rest. You're...making peace with the past. And I admire that."

"You do?"

"Yes. I think you want to clear out all that old garbage between us for good and all. And now that I'm over my initial suspicions I think that's terrific. Because then we can have a chance to be—"

"Yeah?" His voice was suddenly gruff.

"Friends," she finished with a shaky smile. Then she asked, "Am I right?"

He smiled in that way only he knew how, a smile that belonged equally on the face of an angel—and on the devil himself. "Absolutely," he said. "That's exactly what I'm after. To put the past to bed for good and all."

Chapter Eleven

Violet didn't leave the office the next day until after 9:00 p.m. By the time she parked her Volvo in the garage and went out through the small side door to reach the back porch, the sky overhead was blue-black and peppered with stars.

Feeling as if she hadn't stopped moving since she'd hit the floor at a run that morning, Violet paused on the steps to take off her glasses and rub at the aching bridge of her nose. She'd switched from contacts to glasses in the afternoon when her eyes began to hurt from strain. But now, after seven hours, the tabs of the glasses were cutting into the sides of her nose, and she found herself almost wishing she'd stuck with the contacts.

When she slipped the glasses back on, she took a moment to stare up through the interlacing branches of the old walnut tree, picking out from habit the huge handle of the Big Dipper and trying to visualize the Greek hero, Hercules, from the faint grouping of stars.

The sight of the night sky, which had looked much the same during the long summer evenings of her girlhood, reminded Violet that she was at home now, and that the frantic day at Windemere and Carruthers had come to an end. There was no need for her to keep running as if she were consistently one appointment behind. Time enough for that tomorrow.

With a sigh, Violet dropped to the bottom porch step and slipped her shoes off her aching feet. She wriggled her toes to work the stiffness out of them and mentally patted herself on the back for a day well spent.

Somehow, thanks in great part to Melinda's efficiency, everything seemed to be working out. Darrell's calendar, for the next few days at least, was virtually clear—while Violet's was jam-packed. On top of appointments, consultations and court dates, there were, as always, pleadings to write and a mountain of depositions and petitions to file with the county clerk. But Violet was reasonably sure that between herself, her secretary and Melinda, they could handle the crushing work load well enough until Darrell returned.

She stared out across the lawn, noticing that the grass had been dug up and then laid back down in a grid pattern that hadn't been there this morning. She grinned. Slow Larkin, sprinkler installer extraordinaire, had obviously been up to his old tricks. And it looked as if he'd completed the backyard in one day, as promised.

As if in response to her thoughts, Violet heard a low hissing sound by the walk near her foot, and then a sprinkler head there erupted in spray—as did the buried heads over the lawn. With a surprised little laugh, Violet jerked back her foot, but not before her toes got wet.

A chuckle answered her laugh from the side of the porch. She glanced toward the sound just as Slow emerged from whatever he'd been doing at the side of the house.

"You're just in time," he announced as he swung a bare foot up on the porch floor and then levered himself over the railing.

She looked at him doubtfully. "Just in time for what?"

He held a small screwdriver, which he pointed at her. "To approve the final settings of your new sprinkler system." He tossed the screwdriver in the air. It turned, end to end, and then he caught it by the handle. "I saw you drive up, so I snuck out the front to turn them on." He pointed over his shoulder. "The controls are on the side of the house."

"I see," she said, thinking that he was like a breath of fresh air, in his jeans and T-shirt and bare feet, after a day spent reasoning with recalcitrant clients and a gruff judge and later, in the library, poring over endless points of law.

Violet wriggled her toes again and massaged her neck a little, stroking the tightened muscles there.

"Long day, huh?" Slow asked.

"Umm-hmm. Where's Lacy?"

"She just went up to take a bath. And she needs it. She and Evan, Jr. helped me with the sprinklers today, which mostly meant that they chased each other down the trenches and threw dirt clods at each other.

Janine Ferris heard them laughing and got up on a chair in her backyard to watch.''

"She couldn't come over?''

"Are you kidding?'' Slow faked a gasp. "And risk the possibility of getting mud on her dress?''

"Oh.'' Violet nodded. "I forgot about that.''

"Anyway, Janine hung over the fence and planned gruesome punishments for Evan and Lacy while the two of them chased around the yard screaming and throwing dirt.''

Violet laughed. "I'm surprised you finished, then—with all the *help,* I mean.''

He gave her a half smile. "I generally manage to do what I say I'll do.'' Violet blinked, wondering if that statement carried more than one meaning. Then he asked gently, "Did you hear anything from Darrell yet?''

She nodded. "He called in this afternoon. His father was out of surgery and in intensive care by then.''

"He's going to be all right?''

"It looks like it.''

"I'm glad.''

"Me, too. Darrell's settled in at a hotel, one that's close to the hospital. He doesn't know yet how long he'll need to stay—a week at least, possibly two. His mother's in pretty bad shape, and he's been told it won't be safe to move his father for a while. He feels that as long as I can manage here he really should just stay with them.''

"That's understandable,'' Slow said.

Violet looked down at her toes. The conversation with Darrell had been strained. She'd started to tell him that she was retracting the promise he'd wrung from her last night because it was so entirely out of line. But Darrell's mind had, naturally, been on his father and mother, and Violet had decided it would probably be more appropriate to have it out with him after he returned, when they could talk face-to-face.

Slow cut into her thoughts, asking briskly, "So what do you think?" He gestured with the screwdriver at the moonlit lawn glistening beneath the mist of sprinkler spray. "Have I got them set too high?"

Violet turned to look where he pointed. "No, I don't think so," she decided after a moment, thinking how utterly delicious it would be to stand beneath a spray like that and let the cool, heavy mist rinse all her cares away. "Hmm," she said to herself.

"*Hmm,* what?" he asked.

"Well." She tipped her head, pretending to weigh the matter thoroughly. "Maybe they should be even higher."

He considered. "I think it's high enough, really. Higher, and you'll be watering the garage and overfilling the fish pond."

She propped her chin on her fist and pretended to study the patterns of spray. "Maybe so. But could you crank it up anyway, just so I can see how high it will go?"

He shrugged. "Why not, if that's what you want. But come around the side with me. I'll show you how to—"

"In a minute," she interrupted him as she stood in her stocking feet and took a few steps along the walk that led to the driveway, which cut across the yard a third of the way from the house. She turned back to him, smiling. "Just do it, Slow. Just crank it up as high as it will go."

She thought she saw a sudden glitter in his eyes, as if he suspected what she was thinking. "You're sure?"

"Positive."

"Okay, it's your sprinkler system." He stood and leaped back over the railing, disappearing from sight.

Violet faced the yard again. And then swiftly, before she could think of how much the raw-silk suit she was wearing had cost her, she darted down the walk, across the driveway and out into the middle of the sweet-smelling sprinkler-sprayed grass.

She stood there, her head tipped up to the moon, and felt the heavy mist on her legs, drenching her stockings and skirt. As Slow worked the controls, the mist rose higher and higher still, over her thighs and hips, dousing her light jacket and soaking the fine fabric of her blouse, so that it clung to the curves of her breasts.

The spray reached her neck and then fell on her face and doused her hair. She threw out her arms and spun in a circle beneath the deluge, her head thrown back and her mouth open to taste the cool spray on her tongue.

"You're nuts, you know it?" A voice laughed from nearby.

Violet stopping spinning, though for a moment the world went right on whirling anyway. Her eyes found him, at the edge of the driveway, watching her through the high, spinning veil of moisture the sprinklers made.

"Oh," she told him, laughing out loud. "It's wonderful. After the day I've had. It's just . . . washing all my troubles away."

"Not to mention ruining your suit."

"It's worth it."

"It is, huh?"

"Absolutely."

She grinned at him from her watery bower. Her hair was plastered to her head and little rivulets ran down her face and under her collar. She was drenched to the skin, and it felt incredible—so gloriously physical, so marvelously free.

She tipped her head back again, letting the water fall on her face, aware of every inch of her body, from the ache in her lower back acquired while poring for hours over the leather-bound volumes in the library, to the way her slip clung to her breasts, to the puckering of her suddenly chilled nipples beneath the cups of her bra.

She swallowed a mouthful of fallen mist. "Umm. Delicious," she announced and lowered her head again to peer through the mist-spattered lenses of her glasses into Slow's waiting gaze. "I'm not crazy, really, Slow," she said softly.

"No?" He watched her intently, his face very still.

"No, just tired. And in need of... refreshment."

"A beer might have been simpler."

"But not half as much fun."

"Fun, huh?" he asked.

"Yes. Fun."

He took a step, so that his right foot and leg up to the knee were within the spinning, wet veil. She looked down at his bare spray-pelted foot. And then back up at him.

Half-teasingly she said, "What do you think you're doing?"

"Coming in. To see just how fun it is."

"Well now, I don't know..." She backed a step toward the fish pond, feeling a twinge of unease.

"What?" He froze.

She decided she was being unnecessarily jumpy. He had no hidden agenda, he only saw her delight and wanted to share in the fun of running in the sprinklers, acting like a couple of kids at nine-thirty at night. She went on with her light banter, "I don't know if I'll let you in."

He grunted, still grinning. "Do you think you can stop me?"

"I could order you to stay out."

"Try it."

She pretended to think about that, reminded of Evan, Jr. and Lacy, two kids playing in the backyard, bickering over who would run the show. "Never mind," she decided. "If you insist on getting yourself drenched, that's your business. Far be it for me to order you not to."

"Smart girl," he said, chuckling, as he stepped into the whirling mist with her.

Violet stood still, a forbidden anticipation curling warmly in her abdomen while the sprinklers cooled her skin. She watched the swirling showers drench him, soaking his shirt so that it molded his chest, weighting the little question mark of hair that always feel over his forehead so that he had to rake it back with his spread fingers.

He still had the screwdriver in his hand. He hefted it and threw it up again so that it cleared the spray, turning end to end, and landed, once more, in his waiting palm. After that, he stuck it in his back pocket and then just stood there, watching her.

"Your suit is ruined." He more mouthed the words than said them.

"You already said that," she whispered back, feeling strangely reverent now. As if, together, they had stumbled upon some magic watery glen, an enchanted place that would dematerialize around them at the first hint of a jarring sound—just the way it had been all those years ago, sitting on the swing.

"What now?" he asked, taking a step toward her.

"I don't know," she answered, moving forward herself, feeling as if, in this moist, beguiling place, some supernatural force was pulling them inexorably nearer and nearer still to each other.

He took another step, and she did, too, and then they stood close enough to touch.

"Your collar's crooked," he murmured.

"Do you really think it matters now?"

"Everything matters," he told her with great solemnity. "Do you want me to straighten it?"

"Well, I . . ." Violet lightly bit her inner lip, wondering just how they had gotten here, almost touching beneath the sprinklers in the middle of her backyard. It was all completely innocent, of course, they knew where they stood with each other. But still . . .

"You have to ask me," he coaxed.

"Ask you?" She felt mesmerized, wonderfully so, by the low, constant hiss that the sprinklers made, and by Slow's eyes that looked so deeply into hers.

"If you want me to straighten your collar. Ask me," he explained.

"Oh." Did she want that? "Yes, I do. Would you please?"

He raised his hand. She waited, trembling a little, as his hand brushed once down the the line of her collar. She felt him, through the soggy weave of her blouse and her wetly clinging slip, felt the back of his knuckles slide down her chest, from the delicate wings of her collarbone to the cleft between her damp breasts.

"There. That's better," he said.

"Thank you."

"You're welcome."

Beneath her wet clothes, her skin burned where it had felt him. She knew her breathing was coming in sharp little pants.

"Anything else?"

"N-no. I suppose not."

"Your glasses are all wet," he reminded her.

"Yes. You're right." She realized then how much the water on the lenses was distorting everything, making it mistier and softer than it already was.

He lifted his hand again. "You'd see better without them—"

She blinked, like a woman trying to wake from a trance. "No, it's all right..." She lifted her hand in a vague warding-off gesture.

Slow caught her wrist. "You're sure?" His grip was so warm in contrast to the cool showers that spun around them. Her arm, where he held it, felt hot, like her lower body. And her heart was thumping so loudly, drowning out the soft drone that the sprinklers made.

I like your glasses, he'd said a few days ago when he'd taken over her house, *because once I get them off you, you do the damnedest things....*

"What...is happening, Slow?" she asked, bewildered. "I thought..."

"What?"

"That this kind of thing wasn't going to happen," she managed in a husky-sounding whisper.

"You did?" That slow grin had started at the corners of his mouth.

"I thought we were going to be...friends."

"We are, aren't we? Becoming friends?" He still held her wrist between them.

She shifted her gaze from his eyes to her wrist. "Would you please let go?"

"Sure." He released her.

They stood, silently regarding each other beneath the sprinklers for a time. Then she said, "I just want to know where we stand, that's all."

"That's easy. In the middle of your backyard, soaking wet."

"This is no joke, Slow..."

He swiped his hair back again and then laughed. "No. It's *fun*, remember?"

"It was fun a minute ago, but then it became...something else."

"What?"

"It became...seductive. It became about sex."

His eyes narrowed, as if he were gauging how much he could say—and how much she could take. "So?"

"So, it's got to stop."

"All right. Then stop it."

Violet stared at him for a moment, baffled beyond measure. Sometimes dealing with him was like trying to pin down the wind.

"Can't you just...be straight with me?" she demanded.

He held out his hands, palms up. "I'm straight, Red. As straight as *you* are."

"You're impossible," she said.

"No more impossible than you."

She longed to strangle him. Instead she threw her head back and growled at the sky. "Argh!" Then she marched around him and straight for the driveway, where she shrugged out of her ruined jacket and attempted halfheartedly to wring out her skirt. Then after wiping her glasses as best she could on the wet sleeve of her shirt, she resettled them on her nose and trekked soggily to the porch steps where she sat down.

After a moment, he followed her out from beneath the sprinklers, sprinting around to the side of the house to turn them off. To Violet, the absence of the sprinklers rang out almost louder than when they'd been hissing full blast. She twisted the hem of her skirt again as she heard the thump to her right that meant Slow had landed on the porch by leaping the railing once more. She studied the puddle her dripping clothes were forming at the base of the steps as he dropped down beside her.

"Red?"

"Hmm?" She didn't look up; she just concentrated on the pool his own dripping clothes made as it trickled into the puddle from hers.

"Look. I think we *are* becoming friends," he said.

"*I* don't know what to think," she muttered back glumly. "Just when I'm sure I have everything figured out, you go and toss me a curve."

"What curve?"

"Out there on the lawn. The way you straightened my collar. That had . . . innuendos. I thought we were done with innuendos."

He made a low sound, halfway between a chuckle and a growl. "What do you want from me, Red?"

"No," she said almost angrily. "The question is, what do *you* want from me?"

"Quit looking at the concrete, damn it," he demanded. "Look me in the eye."

"All right." She lifted her gaze and glared right at him. "Now tell me. What do you want?"

"Let me put it this way," he said. "I don't want anything that you don't want to give."

"Really?"

"Yeah."

"But what you're saying, obliquely, is that *if* I want to give it, you'd be willing."

"Gee whiz," he teased. "There you go using those big words again. Are you hiding behind those big words, Red?"

"I think you know what 'oblique' means," she said.

He grunted. "Then stop *being* oblique and say what you mean."

"All right." She paused to gather her courage. And then she blurted, "Do you want to make love with me or not?"

He looked at her for a moment, at all of her, from her soggy red hair to the puddle at her feet. Then he said, "You're damn straight I want to make love with you."

A tiny gasp escaped her. "But I thought—"

"What?"

"Well, I mean, you haven't *done* anything—even though you could have, any number of times the past few days." He laughed then. She spoke sharply, "Stop laughing. I don't see what's so funny."

He shook his head. Then he said, "Well, neither have you, Red."

"Neither have I what?"

"*Done* anything."

She really was getting angry, she realized. He seemed to think this was all so utterly amusing. "What exactly am I supposed to *do*, for heaven's sake?" she hissed.

He leaned back on the top step, thinking the question over. "Well, you could have tried to kiss me once or twice," he suggested. "Or at least made an opportunity now and then to touch me—you know, kind of brush against me. Just to let me know you're interested."

Violet gaped at him, totally confused. She'd started out to try to explain how she only intended to be friends with him and ended up getting instructions on how she might be able to seduce him if she played her cards right.

Pure frustration finally loosened her tongue, and she heard herself saying things that she might have been wiser not to frankly reveal. "What are you telling me?" she demanded. "That you didn't notice how I go weak in the knees every time you walk by? That you hadn't the slightest idea what it's like for me, after...the things we did together once, to have you here in my house—half-naked most of the time, looking at me through those baby blues of yours and ready at a moment's notice to—" she faltered and then found the words "—pull out your screwdriver and screw in whatever's loose!"

"Red . . ." he said tenderly, reaching out a hand.

She batted it away. "Don't touch me. Just answer me."

"I am, if you'll listen."

"Fine, I'm listening." She gripped the lip of the step she was sitting on and waited for him to speak.

"Okay," he said. "Let's put it this way. The attraction's still there. For both of us. You want me, and I want you. In bed, naked, just like it was once."

Violet swallowed convulsively. Heat flooded through her midsection at the image that flashed through her mind: the two of them in his bedroom in the deserted gingerbread Victorian house where he'd been raised.

In the vivid scene from her memory they lay naked, facing each other on sweat-dampened sheets. His slow breathing played over her face. "Stay inside me," she'd begged him, wrapping her top leg around him and holding him within. "We'll do it again."

"You'll kill me." He'd laughed, the sound husky and low.

"Yes, with love." She'd pressed herself tighter to him, as if she could absorb him, take the whole of him into herself and never let him go.

He'd groaned and started to move then, and her own hips had answered his, and the beautiful rhythm of love began anew...

"Would you say that's a... fair assessment of the situation?" Slow asked from the darkness beside her now. "That we still want each other?"

Violet shook her head, clearing it of forbidden memories. As she forced her mind back to the here and now, she noticed that the heat in her abdomen had spread to every inch of her body. Her face flamed and her breasts felt heavy and tender, as if they longed for a man's touch.

And not just any man's touch. She wanted Slow Larkin's touch. As well as the moist heat of his lips and tongue, taking her nipples in his mouth, sucking them, driving her wild with desire as only he knew how.

"Red? Are you going to answer me?"

Violet, who had been staring straight ahead, not daring to look at him just then, forced herself to meet his eyes, which seemed to glow the way cats' eyes do in the dark. Violet was poignantly grateful for the dark then, for the fact that the porch light behind them wasn't on. Slow might read her carnal hunger in her expression, but at least he couldn't see the sensual flush that suffused every inch of her skin.

"Yes," she said. "I think it's . . . safe to say that the attraction's still there." *Safe?* a voice in her head scoffed. What in heaven and earth could be called *safe* about the feelings she had for Slow Larkin?

"But you don't want to give in to it, right?" he asked.

She cleared her throat, feeling suspicious. What was he leading up to? She said warily, "That's exactly right."

He nodded. "You have certain plans for your life, and they don't include me. And you're not the type to make love just because you want to. For you, there has to be more."

"Right."

He shrugged. "So you haven't given me any up-front signals that you want me in your bed. And I've accepted that. And whatever either of us may secretly desire, nothing's going to happen unless you tell me, in no uncertain terms, that being naked in bed with me is something you want. With no doubts and no hesitations." His teeth flashed in the darkness. "Like I said out there on the lawn. You have to ask me. You have to say what you want, otherwise . . ."

"What?"

He was still grinning. "Otherwise, nothing. You're safe from me. I'll probably continue to wander around in the morning without my shirt. That's the way I am. And I suppose we won't escape a few *innuendos* now and then. Innuendos tend to happen between men and women who want each other but refuse to do anything about it." He stood then and looked down at her. "Good enough?"

Violet stared up his wet black jeans, over the clinging T-shirt and into his shadowed face. She was remembering the way she'd felt when she first saw him again a few days before—like Alice down the rabbit hole. She was thinking that the conversation they'd just shared would have gone over just fine at the Mad Hatter's tea party. "Okay," she said. "Yes. Fine."

"Then we're clear with each other?" he prompted gently.

"Yes. Nothing's going to happen unless I come right out and ask for it."

He nodded. "You got it."

"And since I'm not going to do that," she went on, "well, nothing's going to happen. What could be more clear than that?"

"Nothing, Red." He chuckled.

She peered up at him, wary again. "What are you laughing about, then?"

"Because for someone who has it all clear in her mind..."

"Yes?"

"You look damn confused." He held out a hand to her. "Now come on inside and get dry."

She let him help her up, telling herself that the way her toes curled at his touch didn't have to mean anything, just as he'd said. It was her choice—and she chose to do nothing about the way he made her feel.

"Did you get to eat?" he asked as he led her inside.

"Just a sandwich, this afternoon."

"I saved you a pork chop."

"You did?"

"You bet."

"Thanks, Slow."

"My pleasure," he said. "Anything for a friend...."

Chapter Twelve

Slow tossed the wrench back in his toolbox and spun the handle on the tap. Water flooded the sink. He spun the handle the other way and the water was cut off, with no leakage.

He nodded to himself. The new washer he'd just put in was fine. Then he glanced at his watch. A quarter of three in the afternoon. Was Red in the office now?

He'd called an hour ago, after leaving Bob Ferris, and had been told she was still at the courthouse but was expected back soon. He wanted to see her, to show her the fifteen hundred square feet of garage he'd just bought. He wanted...what? For her to like it?

Slow slammed the lid shut on his toolbox and then washed his hands. After that, he wiped the taps free of the evidence that he'd been working there. He was feeling like an idiot, really. After he shook hands on the deal with Bob, he'd thought that showing her the place would be a good excuse to see her in the middle of the day.

And once the idea got lodged in his head, he couldn't get it out. It stuck there, playing over and over, like a record with a bad scratch in it. So he'd called her from a phone booth.

And then, when she wasn't there, he'd rushed back to the house feeling nervy as a tomcat in mating season. He made himself a sandwich, wishing Lacy hadn't gone over to Glory's for the day. Her company would have kept his mind off Red.

He'd noticed the leak in the tap while he was rinsing off the plate from his solitary lunch. He'd rushed right over to the hardware store down the street to find a replacement. He thought that by the time he'd put in the new washer, he'd have forgotten all about heading over to Windemere and Carruthers and talking Red into going for a little drive with him.

Slow yanked open the refrigerator and got himself a cold one. Then he sprawled in a kitchen chair and stared blindly out the side window at the white picket fence that merged into a seven-foot redwood affair in the backyard. He stared at the tall gate that stood in front of the driveway, idly pondering the prospect of getting her a gate on rollers that could be opened and shut electronically so she wouldn't have to get in and out of her car to deal with it every time she wanted to go somewhere.

Slow let out a short bark of laughter and took a long pull of his beer. Maybe he was getting a little carried away with all this handyman stuff. He was fixing things like crazy—more to keep his mind off a certain redhead than to impress her with how great he was around the house.

In fact, his little plot to exact a passionate revenge was kind of turning around on him. He often forgot exactly what he was supposed to be after from her. He found himself saving her something to eat when she got home simply because he knew she'd be too tired to think of cooking. Or he would try to coax a soft smile from her without even considering that making her laugh would make her like him more, which would get him closer to being in her bed. Hell, most of the time he wanted to make her smile just for the pleasure it gave him to see her face light up.

It had been almost a week since Darrell had left. Red said that it could be as long as another week before the other man returned. Which was just fine with Slow in one sense: it gave him a clearer field with Red.

Once he'd learned that Darrell's parents would eventually be all right, Slow had even let himself gloat a little over the situation. This time around, fate seemed to be on his side, taking his rival out of the running for a solid two weeks.

However, there were drawbacks to having Red's law partner on emergency leave. As a result of Darrell's absence, Red's schedule was so packed that Slow never set eyes on her until at least seven at night. This past weekend she'd gone into the office both days.

But she'd said last night that things were settling down a little, that she pretty much had it under control. And since Darrell was sure he'd be back within a week, she'd been able to start filling his calendar again, taking a little of the load off her own shoulders by postponing what she could until he returned.

Slow drained the last of his beer and then stomped on the can. He tossed the flat cylinder of metal into the bag under the sink where Red put cans for recycling.

Then he wandered out to the back porch and hitched a thigh up on the railing. He stared at the huge purple clusters of flowers that lined the fence between the Ferrises' and Red's. Last night when they'd sat out here together, Red had told him the name of those flowers—hydrangeas, that was it.

Right after she'd told him that, he'd put his arm along the back of the swing behind her. And she'd given him one of her looks.

"Slow..." She'd said it pleadingly, begging him to kiss her, begging him not to at the same time.

He loved to watch her mouth form his name, watch her eyes go cloudy, like sea foam. Her lips had stayed slightly parted after whispering the *w* in his name. He could have kissed her then, he knew it. Just as he could have a thousand times since he'd taken up residence in her house. Lacy had already gone upstairs to bed, so there would have been nothing to make it awkward, had the kiss gone on to something more. Beneath the placket of his jeans, he'd been hard as a randy kid, just from looking at her mouth and thinking of taking it with his own.

Slow shifted on the railing. Damn. It was bad and getting worse. He went around with a bulge in his jeans most of the time now.

But he'd sworn he wouldn't make love to her unless she asked him to. And in spite of the pleading look in her eyes, and the way her mouth went soft as velvet when she said his name, she hadn't asked. And he hadn't taken.

They were *friends*. Slow made a sound that was half laugh and half groan.

Then he stood and leaped the railing. He wanted to see her. In the middle of the day for once. And he *was* going to see her. Right now.

The intercom on Violet's desk buzzed. She smiled at Wilma Mateo, who sat across from her twisting the frayed strap of her black vinyl purse. "One moment," she reassured her nervous client. Then she spoke into the intercom. "Yes?"

"Someone named . . . Slow Larkin is here," Roger, the receptionist for the six lawyers in the building, said. His voice sounded doubtful.

Violet smiled and felt her heart pleasantly pick up in rhythm. But then she frowned, wondering if something might be wrong. She'd received the message that he'd called earlier, but it had said not to bother calling back. She'd wondered if everything was okay, then concluded that whatever it was could wait until she got home. Obviously that wasn't so.

"I'll come out," she said.

She gave another smile to Wilma Mateo. "There's someone I need to speak to now. But I'll be right back. All right?"

"Okay." Wilma nodded, her dark eyes wide as saucers. "I'll wait."

Even in her preoccupation with what might be wrong at home, Violet felt empathy for her lushly pretty, soft-spoken client. Wilma was engaged in a custody battle with the father of her illegitimate child. The man had recently married a well-to-do woman who couldn't have children of her own. Tomorrow Wilma went before the judge, and she was terrified. Not only of losing her child but of the whole intimidating legal process. Violet felt they had a good case, if only Wilma could survive her own fear.

"It's going to be fine, Wilma," Violet said. "We have a good case."

"I know." Wilma clutched her purse tighter and forced a brave smile. "You go on. I'll be right here when you get back."

Violet left her office for the reception area, where Slow stood waiting by the water cooler.

"What is it?" Her concern was evident in her voice. "I got the message that you called, but it said not to call back."

"That's right."

"Is something wrong? Is Lacy okay?"

"Everything's fine."

"Then what?"

He grinned at her and then took her arm, pulling her around the cooler and into the short hall. He found the door to the copy room, peeked inside to see it was empty and tugged her in there.

She laughed because it was so good to see him. And then she felt silly; she saw him every day. "Slow, I'm with a client..."

"I know, I know—I want to show you something."

"What?"

"Can you get away?"

She opened her mouth to say no, but he looked so hopeful that she couldn't quite get her mouth around the word. And, actually, Wilma Mateo was her last appointment for the day. She'd planned to spend the rest of it on paperwork, which, as usual, should have been done yesterday.

But then she *had* been working like a demon for the past week. And maybe it would be good for her to take the tail end of the afternoon off for a change.

"Well, I..."

"Come on," he implored.

"I have to finish up with a client. A half hour, probably."

"I'll wait."

"Okay, then."

"Terrific." He was beaming. From a high west-facing window the sun slanted in, cutting a swath of brightness across his cheek. His eyes looked lighter than she'd ever seen them, full of frank anticipation at sharing with her whatever he was taking her to see.

She was standing with a hand on his arm, smiling up at him. Without stopping to think, she brushed his sun-warmed cheek with her lips. "Half an hour. Roger will give you coffee—if you'd like."

"Okay," he said. She turned to leave. "Red?"

Pausing in the doorway to the hall, she glanced back at him. "Yes?"

He looked bemused, and then he touched his cheek where she'd kissed him, as if the feel of her lips still lingered there. A flush bloomed upward over Violet's face, staining her features a warm pink. The brush of her lips on his cheek had been little more than a peck. But still, it was the first kiss she'd given him in eleven years.

She touched her mouth, since it suddenly tingled. He grinned at her.

"Never mind," he said.

"A half hour," she managed to whisper.

He nodded. "A half hour."

She fled down the hallway, feeling foolish and giddy and about sixteen years old.

Twenty-eight minutes later, they sat in Slow's black Chevy and were headed down Main Street, and then turning on Union, on the way to Broad Street, she supposed.

"Your client looked scared," Slow said casually, keeping his eyes on the road as he drove.

"She is."

Slow glanced over at her. "She also looks poor. Not like your classic Windemere and Carruthers-type client at all."

"She's not, I guess. Her case is *pro bono*—no charge to the client. I try to take on at least ten percent *pro bono* cases. They're referred through the Voluntary Legal Services Program office in Auburn. It's important, I think. To give back to the community." Her voice was a tad defensive, and Slow noticed immediately.

He raised a hand from the steering wheel—a wooden wheel that looked huge in comparison to the smaller ones in modern cars. "Hey. I think that's great. You don't have to justify giving a little help to someone who needs it."

Violet gave a humorless chuckle. "I guess I'm a little touchy about it. Darrell has never liked my spending time on cases that don't pay—and while my father was alive, he vetoed the idea whenever I brought it up." Violet cleared her throat, deciding it was probably wiser not to say anything that sounded critical of Darrell *or* Clovis. She quickly changed the subject. "This car runs like a dream, Slow."

He accepted the safer subject without comment, explaining with a smug grin, "Just suspension components. Monroe Gas-Matric shocks."

Violet nodded, her mouth open. "Right."

"What I'm saying—" he braked at the stop sign before they crossed the freeway at the foot of Broad Street "—is I rebuilt this car from the frame up. It's not a true restoration. I made a few improvements, to give me a comfortable everyday vehicle. I put in an air conditioner—as well as an AM-FM cassette player." He pulled a tape from the glove box and stuck it in the cassette player in the dash. A husky male voice singing a soft rock tune filled the car.

"Nice," Violet said. Outside, it was near ninety degrees, but the vintage car, with the windows up and the air conditioner on, was as comfortable as Violet's living room on a crisp fall afternoon.

They had crossed the highway and then turned right onto Sacramento Street, then left on Clay.

"Where *are* we going?" she wondered aloud.

"Almost there." He turned onto Prospect and then pulled into a lot with a garage on it that had obviously once been a gas station. The concrete blocks where the pumps had stood were still there.

"Wait here," he instructed. He left the engine idling and went in through the glassed-in office area. Violet watched as the metal roll-up door beyond the car's hood began to rise.

When the door was all the way up, Slow reappeared, sliding in behind the wheel. He drove the black car into the open bay. Then he shifted into Park and pulled the key from the ignition.

"Wait a minute." She laughed. "I think I get it. You've found a garage."

He grinned back. "Come on. I'll show you around." They got out of the car.

Slow led her around the dim, cool space, pointing out the pit for working beneath the car in the next-door bay, then explaining that the steel-topped work-benches were much better than wood, and that the air compressor was in fine shape.

Violet nodded, looking appreciative, as he indi-cated tool boards and shelves and hundreds of differ-ent-sized drawers. After a quick glance at the office, the small rest room and the storage area behind, they returned to the far bay where Slow's car waited. There, Slow hoisted himself up on a table by the passenger door, and Violet leaned against the car.

"So what do you think?"

"It's great," she said. But she was wondering about a few things, and her ambivalence must have been there in her voice.

"But what?" he prompted.

"Oh, I don't know. I guess I'm still a little con-fused about exactly what it is you plan to do here."

"Restore cars," he said in an isn't-it-obvious tone.

"But, Slow, I've read the articles about what you've done down in Southern California..."

"I'm flattered," his voice tried to tease, but in his eyes there was a warning look. She was pursuing a subject he didn't want to discuss.

"The point is..."

"Yeah?"

"Isn't this—" she put out a hand to indicate the dim garage around them "—a little like going backward for you?"

He looked away. "Maybe I want to...get back to what it's all about. Taking a battered piece of junk and, all by my lonesome, turning it into a living slice of the past.''

She shook her head. ''I don't know...''

He jumped down from the bench. ''You don't have to know.'' He sounded almost angry. ''What matters to you is when I'm getting out of your hair. And it won't be long now. Bob Ferris has two houses to show me tomorrow, and as soon as I choose one, me and Lacy are out of your life for good.'' He turned to walk past her, as if he wanted to get away.

''Slow, I...'' She put a restraining hand on his arm and realized her mistake immediately in the way his muscles clenched.

''What?'' He turned to her. ''What do you want? What the *hell* do you want?''

Violet gaped at him, trying to absorb what had happened. In questioning the logic of his plans, she'd hit a nerve with him. And suddenly everything had changed, shifted. All his lazy humor and his patient control were gone. A moment ago they had been friends, aware of the attraction between them but reasonably comfortable with it, too. Now the air between them crackled, thick with static, as if a storm was coming.

It's going to happen, she thought incredulously. It's going to *really* start now, here, in this cool cave of a garage, where the smell of gasoline and oil still lingers—in *his* place. And it's going to end in mine. In my room. In my bed. As both of us want it to, as both of us have known it would since the moment I opened the door and found him standing on my front porch the Saturday before last.

''I...'' She let go of his arm and backed up a step, though she knew it was futile to try to escape now.

"Yeah?" He moved in, hemming her against the car. His breath was agitated, causing warm gusts on her face. And he was so close she could feel his chest moving in and out against her breasts.

"I...you know I'll miss you," she murmured weakly in a final attempt to stop this madness that was claiming her, to say something that would soothe him and perhaps make him back away. "You and Lacy, too..." His mouth hovered above hers. She wondered, as a wild thing trapped in a snare might wonder, how she'd gotten here, her lips inches from his, caught in the fulcrum of his damning gaze, and longing, *hungering,* to feel his mouth on hers.

Yes, that was what she wanted: his mouth on hers. But that was *wrong,* and she knew it. It would only lead to trouble. And there was that absurd promise to Darrell to consider, too. A promise she never should have made, perhaps, but she still felt it binding her, nonetheless.

"You'll miss me, huh?"

"Yes," she swallowed, convulsively. "Yes, I will..."

"How much will you miss me, Red?"

"I..."

"Why don't you show me, Red?"

"Slow, you said..." Her voice trailed off, stolen by her own desperation.

"What?"

She managed bravely, "That if I didn't ask for it..."

"Forget what I said. Forget everything." At that moment he destroyed her last weak attempts to resist the heat between them. He did it with the simplest and most primitive of movements. He ground his hips against hers. "Forget it all," he commanded huskily. "Except for this..."

Chapter Thirteen

Slow felt her barely contained moan as he rubbed his hardness against the cove of her thighs, pressing into her, seeking to claim her through the skirt of the classy linen suit she wore.

"Oh, Lord, Slow..." she murmured.

He knew, with a hot flash of male triumph, that beneath her skirt and her stockings, her body was readying itself for him. He sensed, exultantly, that he could have entered her right then, and she could have taken him, without a twinge of discomfort, with nothing but a long, voluptuous sigh....

His lips were a fraction from hers. He taunted her with her own needs. "Remember, Red. Remember how it was for us..."

"I can't..."

"You can," he insisted. "You always could. Anytime, Red. Now..."

He looked into her eyes, glazed with wanting him, and he would have smiled if his hunger for her hadn't been so great. She was wearing her contacts instead of her glasses, and that worked in his favor, because he would have taken her glasses off before he kissed her. And the few seconds' pause that would have created might have given her time to change her mind.

But now, in this cool dim cavern of space he owned, with her buttocks pressed against the door of his car and his hips grinding their promise into hers, there was nothing, no action, that marked off the moment when his lips covered hers.

It happened. He took her mouth. Or she took his. It would have been hard to say which.

And the moment their lips touched, Violet groaned aloud. He groaned, too, starved for her as he was. And she sighed, opening, taking his tongue inside. Then she lifted her arms, to clasp his head, to splay her fingers in his hair and hold him still for her hungry mouth so she could kiss him some more.

He felt his own heart kicking hell against his ribs, as if it wanted to get out, get closer to her. Her hands left off holding his head in place to glide down and over his shoulders. He felt her, loving it, after all these years, as she relearned his body, her soft hands gliding over the muscles of his shoulders, and then slipping down to his chest.

Then she was clutching him all over, her hungry touch running up and down his sides, questing, seeking. He moaned into her mouth as she yanked his shirt free of his jeans and rucked it up over his belly so that she could feel his bare skin.

And then he could wait no longer to touch her in return. He put his hands on her slim shoulders, bunching her jacket, sliding it off and down her arms.

Violet, for her part, was vaguely aware that Slow tossed her jacket on the roof of the car behind her. But then every sense she possessed was on his hands again as he pulled her blouse free of her skirt and clutched for her bare waist, only to find she was wearing a slip.

He made a frustrated sound in his throat, one that echoed inside her head since their mouths were still hungrily joined. She realized that he wanted to feel her bare skin against his own, and that the slip was foiling his need. She groaned, too, wanting the same thing. After all these years. Just to feel him. Against her. Flesh to flesh. Again. Always....

Desperately she pulled on the slip, and he understood her aim and helped her. They slid it from under her skirt, up out of the way. And then he was working the front clasp of her bra.

Her breasts swung free and he cupped them, sighing into her mouth, a grateful, tender sound that made her smile. Then he pulled her close, chest to breast, and the wonder of being crushed against him, feeling him, *touching* his body with her own after so long, made her want to cry for happiness and scream for joy.

"Slow," she sighed. "Oh, yes, at last..."

And Slow took the sounds into his mouth as he rubbed himself against her breasts, savoring her small aroused whimper as her hard little nipples were made harder still by the rough stimulation of rubbing against the wiry hair on his chest.

Slow felt like a man who'd wandered, lost and alone, for over a decade, now sighting at last the lights of home. Her breasts, her satiny belly, the long, slender clasp of her arms—all were his, his alone, to know and to glory in.

He felt the hot pounding in his blood, pushing him toward possession of what was his, demanding fulfillment in the soft heat of her body. He knew the urgent need to take her now because she would receive him, to bunch her skirt and tear her stockings and get inside her before the sweet madness of her total surrender might pass and leave him thwarted at heaven's door.

But some scrap of sanity did remain in him. He hadn't lived thirty-three years on his own terms without learning a little about the price a man pays for blindly taking what he wants. The bay door was still open, he realized dimly. And he didn't want their first time, after all these years, to be too quick or too awkward.

Here, there was no place for them except the cold concrete floor, or the hood of his car, or maybe the back seat. It would be rough and frantic, rather than slow and tender and achingly sensual, as he wanted it to be.

No, he decided with an internal groan. It couldn't be now, it couldn't be here . . .

From some deep resource of will he hadn't before known he possessed, Slow took her by the shoulders and lifted his head.

Violet, dazed with desire, raised heavy lids to look at him. She realized, through the sensual fog of her need, that he was saying, "Not here," or something like that. He took his body away from her, pulling back a step.

His hooded gaze fell on her bare breasts, so full and white in the dim light, the nipples hard little pebbles jutting out from beneath the silky tangle of her bunched-up slip. He murmured something dark and low, deep in his throat. Then, after pulling down his own shirt, he gently began to reclasp her bra, tuck her slip back into her skirt and rebutton her blouse that had slid half off her shoulders.

Violet stood unmoving beneath his hands, except to turn her head a little and look out the bay door at the sun-bright street, where anyone passing by might have glanced in and seen what they'd been doing mere minutes ago.

"There," he said tenderly when he'd finished rebuttoning her blouse. He reached behind her and found her jacket and gave it to her. She took it in numb hands, folding it over one arm and looking down at it for a moment, to put off looking at him.

He waited, for a time, and then he tipped her chin up with a finger. His eyes smiled into hers, both desire and compassion curling like twin tendrils of smoke in their depths. The anger he'd shown before was gone now, as if the elemental intensity of what had just happened had washed it away. As if he could afford, once again, to be humorous and patient and gentle with her.

"Come on," he coaxed when she remained painfully mute. "It's not the end of the world. Just think of it as...a kiss that got a little out of hand. It happens between men and women all the time."

Violet gazed into his eyes, still feeling dazed, and heard herself repeating his words. "Right. A kiss that got out of hand, not the end of the world at all, happens all the time..." A sound escaped her, a short laugh that was more like a sob. She tried to turn her head away, but he had slipped his whole hand beneath her chin now and held her steady, so she had to look at him.

"Damn it, Red," he said through suddenly clenched teeth, the hot intensity of a few moments ago creeping back into his eyes. "Did you think we could go on forever, not touching, playing in the sprinklers and swinging on the porch swing?"

"No, I..."

"What?" The word had a torn sound, as if it hurt him to say it. "Talk to me."

"I suppose not," she admitted, and he released her chin. She looked down, and then forced herself to face him again. "But until this..." She held out a palm, indicating what had just happened as if it were an actual object a few feet away. "Until today, it was still possible to lie to myself. But now..."

"Yeah?" His voice was hopeful, hurt and tender. "Now what?"

"Now I know—and you know—what will happen sooner or later. And even if you try to be kind and say it was only a kiss that got out of hand, we both know it was much more. It was...a line, and we just crossed it. And there's no going back from it. We'll end up in my bed together. It's just a matter of time."

His face was stark, free of his previous gentle pretense. She saw the frank hunger in his eyes, the same hunger she felt.

He nodded. "When, then?" he said.

"I don't know," she answered. "I need some time. To...fully accept it. And I made a promise to Darrell that—"

His jaw tensed. "What promise? You never said you'd marry him—did you?"

"No, I didn't."

"Then what the hell promise do you mean?"

"I said I wouldn't . . . let anything happen between you and me until after he returned and he and I could talk."

"About what?" He was angry all over again, almost as angry as before he'd forced her up against the car and demanded the response from her that only he knew how to claim.

"Slow, please don't be like this. I know you and Darrell have never liked each other much . . ."

He made a scoffing sound. "Say it like it is, Red. We hate each other's guts."

"Slow . . ." She struggled to make him comprehend. "He's my friend. He's always been my friend. He was right beside me when my father died, and he was right there with a shoulder to cry on when you and I broke up eleven years ago—"

"I'll just bet he was," Slow muttered darkly.

"Look. I don't want to hurt him any more than I have to. Please understand."

Slow looked at her a long time, and finally his hard gaze softened a little. "Until he comes back, that's how long you want? Until he comes back and you can tell him about you and me?"

She held her head high. "Yes."

"And then you'll come to me?" Slow asked.

There was only one possible answer now. Violet gave it in an even, steady voice.

"Yes. I'll come to you, and ask you to make love with me. Just like we agreed."

Chapter Fourteen

The drive back to the house from the garage passed in silence. So much had happened since he'd picked her up at the office, and both of them had said all they wanted to say right then.

Soon after they arrived home, Lacy Jay came bouncing in. Tacitly, Slow and Violet focused their attention on the child, urging her to talk about her day as the three of them fixed a meal of steaks and salads and baked potatoes, topped off with rocky-road ice cream for dessert.

During the evening, Slow remained low-keyed and subdued. He did nothing, in word or gesture, to challenge her or remind her that she would soon be his. But still, to Violet, it seemed as if the sensual pact between them shimmered in the very air around them, rising up like heat ripples from hot asphalt on a sweltering summer day.

Merely being in the same room with him created in her a constant state of agonized anticipation—which was the main reason she decided to turn in even earlier than usual. She was exhausted from all that had happened. But even beyond her fatigue, she held out a vain hope that as soon as she escaped to her room, she might be able to relax a little.

Outside, the sun had just finished setting when she rose from the couch, where she'd been sitting staring grimly at the television.

"I think I'll go on to bed," she announced in a voice that she tried to make as bland as white bread.

"Tired, huh?" Slow was sitting in the big chair, scanning the latest issue of a car magazine, flipping the pages idly, and he tossed off the mundane question without looking up.

"Yes," Violet agreed. "It's been . . . quite a day."

Lacy craned her head around from her standard position—stretched out on the floor in front of the television. "Night, Violet."

"Night, Lacy," Violet responded, and took the first step toward the haven of her room.

She didn't quite make it unscathed. Because Slow glanced up at her, and the sudden flare of heat she saw in his eyes licked out and burned her, right down to her curling toes. "Sleep well, Red," he said, the words a verbal equivalent of a long, slow caress.

"Yes." Violet cleared her throat, feeling her face flame. "I will. Thank you. Good night." She fled to her room, as if pursued by fiends.

Violet *was* pursued, actually. By the demons of her own desire. She lay in bed wearing her shorty pajamas, unable to bear the weight of even a sheet on her fevered body, feeling the fabric of the pajamas against her breasts as a stimulant, making her nipples erect.

She dreamed of Slow's mouth, and of his body rubbing against hers. And she'd never been so grateful in her life as when she rose the next morning and found that he, as usual, was still in bed. She wouldn't have to see him again until evening brought her home. She forced her mind to thoughts of Wilma Mateo and her battle to keep her child.

The day began well because Wilma Mateo won. She was granted continuing custody, while the natural father received certain limited visitation rights, to which Wilma agreed.

After hearing the decision, Violet and Wilma left the courthouse together. On the steps outside, beneath the bright morning sun, Wilma grabbed Violet and hugged her.

"Thank you, thank you! I can never tell you," Wilma whispered fiercely in her ear, "how much I thank you...."

Violet felt the tears rising in her eyes, thinking that *this* was what her work was all about and remembering what Slow had said yesterday. *You don't have to justify giving a little help to someone who needs it....*

Strange, how Slow seemed to understand better than anyone the things that really mattered to her, whether it be the sounds of laughter and life around her, or the necessity to use her abilities to help people who needed it.

Violet hastily brushed her tears away and took Wilma by the shoulders. "It was a fair decision, nothing more. You give that little boy a big hug for me, okay?"

"I will," Wilma agreed. Violet walked the other woman to her battered car and waved as she pulled away.

The rest of the day was busy but routine. Violet threw herself into the daily grind with grim determination. In a way, she was hiding from Slow, and from the staggering reality of the agreement they'd made.

At work she didn't have to look at him, and have him look at her, and be made constantly aware that, very soon, they would be lovers. At work she could hold the inevitable at a mental distance for a while.

But eventually the day did end. And she did go home. And he was there.

And for that night and the next two nights to follow, they lived in a sort of sensual purgatory, where the very air seemed thick with unspoken desires, where his eyes hungered and hers yearned in response. But neither made a move.

Or said a thing.

On Friday, Violet visited her doctor to be fitted for a contraceptive device. She went home that night with the small cap in its case in her purse. It made her feel good about herself, to take care of that, at the same time as it made the fact that they would soon make love even more real to her than before.

At home the tension increased. Violet knew that Slow waited, as she waited, for Darrell to return and set them both free to claim what they wanted—the touch, the response, the passion and the fulfillment.

What Violet *didn't* know was the extra agonies Slow suffered during those endless hours. Because during that time, Slow Larkin at last admitted to himself that he'd been beaten by his own game.

He relived, over and over, those shattering moments in the dim garage when he'd touched her and tasted her—at last, after all these years. He felt again the lush weight of her breasts in his hands, the hungry little whimpers she made into his mouth that told him she wanted him, however she could have him, whenever he said.

And now she would be his, the sweet secrets of her body his to reveal and to claim. It was only a matter of days—perhaps hours if Darrell returned earlier than assumed.

Slow would have her body. Just as he'd planned that first night when she was supposed to have been off somewhere telling the other man *yes*.

Slow would have her willing and hungry, just as he'd intended. He'd won his very special revenge.

But the problem was that now he wanted much more than her body. He wanted her trust, and he wanted honesty between them.

And he wanted her love.

He understood that now. Maybe he'd wanted her love from the first, but had been too scared she might not give it to him to admit that her heart was what he'd been after all along.

Now he knew better. Because she was a woman made for loving. He'd made himself forget that after she sent him away years ago, but it was impossible not to learn it all over again, being around her day in and day out.

Sometime during his campaign to break down her defenses, she had demolished all of his. In a way, now it was even worse than eleven years ago, when he had loved her with an all-consuming need. Now he consciously understood just how much more there was to want about her than the incredible way her body caught fire from his.

He couldn't get out of his mind the way she was with Lacy—affectionate and humorous, tender and kind. And the way she gave away her legal services to people who couldn't afford to pay for them. And the way she really listened when they talked together, and the subtle humor that was always there beneath her surface reserve.

He used to wonder what it had been about her that could have made the two boys she grew up with each want her so desperately in their own separate ways. She was no great beauty, and her manner was quiet, almost shy.

Now he no longer wondered. She was good and kind, sweet and funny. She *cared* about other people, and she made her corner of the world a better place to be. Any man she took to stand beside her would have all a man could ever want—nights that lit up the sky and days of joy and laughter.

And now his whole scheme to get her into bed made him sick to his stomach whenever he thought about it. She was worth so much more than that, and she deserved so much better.

Every day he woke intending to tell her everything as soon as she got home from work that night. And every night, when she'd walk in the door and his desire for her would hit him like a punch to the gut, he'd know that there was no way he was going to say a word. Not until he'd been in her bed at least once more.

It was wrong, and he knew it. But if she sent him away again once she learned how he'd manipulated her, he at least wanted to have his little piece of heaven to remember when he left.

Wednesday, Thursday, Friday. Somehow the days crept by.

Darrell called nightly—to check on how Violet was doing at work without him, he said. But both Violet and Slow knew that the other man was checking *up* as well as *in,* making sure that Violet remained true to the unfair promise he'd dragged from her.

Saturday Violet planned to go into the office at ten or so—well before Slow came downstairs. She probably could have stayed home. Things were basically under control by then. But it was easier, given the sensual powder keg they were sitting on, if they spent as much time as they could apart.

However Glorianna showed up at eight-thirty wearing a red jumpsuit and tennis shoes, her arm through Arthur's, who looked very sporty in a golfing hat and plaid shorts.

"Dress casually, my darlings!" Glorianna announced as she swept into the house. "We're going to the state fair!"

Immediately Lacy Jay began leaping around the entrance hall. "Wow, great! Can I ask Evan, Jr., please, Glory? Can Evan come, too?"

Glorianna agreed that Evan, Jr. could come—as well as Janine and Callie Ferris. Lacy Jay made a face, but then grudgingly conceded that Janine ought to be invited, too.

"But I'm going to tell her she's got to wear something that can get dirty, okay? 'Cause I can't have fun if she's gonna be whining every time she gets a spot on her dress."

"All right, my sweet," Glorianna soothed. "We'll go invite her and her sister, and Evan, too, right now. But I think it would be best if you allow *me* to suggest the proper attire. Fair enough?" Lacy nodded, and Glorianna turned to give Arthur a tender smile. "There's coffee in the kitchen, I can smell it, my angel. I'm sure Violet won't mind if you help yourself. Lacy Jay and I will return posthaste." She flicked a glance at Violet. "My love, why don't you go wake Slow?"

"Well, Mother, I—"

But Lacy Jay had already pulled Glorianna out the door.

"Wonderful. Coffee..." the soft-spoken Arthur murmured and disappeared into the butler's pantry beyond the stairs.

Violet stood alone in the hallway for a moment, thinking that there was nothing to stop her from simply not doing what her mother had requested she do. It was no big deal. When Glorianna and Lacy Jay returned, one of them could wake the night owl.

But somehow one foot was on the bottom stair, and then she was climbing to the upper floor, knowing she was doing this for one reason only—to get a glimpse of him in bed.

The door was ajar. It didn't squeak when she pushed it open all the way. She'd been just about to shower when Glorianna arrived, so she was still wearing her light summer robe and slippers. The slippers were nearly silent on the floor and muffled even more on the old rug that covered most of the room.

Slow lay on the high double bed, on his stomach, the covers at his waist. She could see the firm curve of his buttocks beneath the blankets. One leg was drawn up, while the other stuck out straight.

His muscled back was fully revealed to her. One arm was bent at the elbow, the hand near his tousled head, the other lay lax at his side. His head was turned away and half-buried in a pillow.

On silent feet Violet reached the side of the bed. And then she just stood there, looking at him, longing to reach out and trace the hard curves and shadowed hollows of his back, to trail her hand down, hook a finger in the blanket and slowly pull it back.

Her breasts ached, her body yearned.

Soon, a voice in her head soothed. *Soon...*

"Slow?" she said gently.

He stirred. "Umm?"

"Slow, wake up..."

He groaned and rolled over, throwing a hand across his eyes. She saw the hair beneath his arm. It seemed incredibly intimate to her to see that. She wanted to put her lips there, and then to trail her tongue down his side, over onto his belly and dip into his navel. She wanted to taste him. All over. Every inch of him.

"What time is it?" he asked from beneath his arm.

"Before nine."

"No one," he growled and then repeated, "*no one* wakes me up before ten-thirty."

"I know, but—"

He didn't let her explain. "No buts. Get lost," he instructed in a sleep-rough whisper, then peeked out at her through weighted lids. "Or get in this bed with me."

Her body quivered at the suggestion, but she stayed where she was. "Don't. It's not fair."

He brought his arm down, rolled his head toward her and smiled. It was a smile so devastatingly sleepy and sexy that she almost leaped across the short distance that separated them and crawled beneath the covers as he'd suggested. "Don't what?" he asked.

"You know..." she said in a hoarse whisper.

"I thought maybe..."

"No. Not yet."

"I see," he said. After that he glanced away for a moment, toward an armoire in the corner. When he looked at her once more, he'd masked the sleepy promise in his eyes somewhat. "Okay. What's up?"

"My mother and Arthur are here. They want to go to the state fair today. Mother and Lacy Jay are out inviting Evan Blaylock and Janine and Callie Ferris right now."

Slow dragged himself upright, careful to pull the blankets with him. She wondered if he was nude beneath the blankets, and then felt her face flushing at the thought.

Violet continued, her voice idiotically breathy. "Mother asked me to get you up. They want to get going. I mean, it's an hour's ride, at least, and unless you get moving, half the day'll be gone before you even reach Sacramento."

He yawned. "Makes sense."

"So you have to get up now."

"I understand."

"Good." Violet smiled at him, and then realized she was more or less behaving like a lovestruck fool. "Well, then..."

"Yeah?"

"I guess that's all."

"I guess so."

"I'll . . . I'll see you downstairs, then."

"Right. Thanks."

"No problem." She whirled, jerkily, and got out of there.

Then she marched straight down the stairs and into her bathroom, where she treated her untamed lust for Slow Larkin with the oldest remedy known to man— a freezing cold shower.

She emerged into the kitchen fully dressed in a simple skirt appropriate for the office on a nonworking day. She learned then that Glorianna fully expected her to go with them.

"Mother, I need to work," Violet argued in as firm a tone as she could summon.

"Nonsense. You'll drop dead if you don't slow down a little. All work and no play makes my daughter a heart attack victim."

Little did Glorianna know, Violet thought grimly. She was a victim of a heart attack, all right, but not the killing kind. Oh, no. Violet's own particular heart attack went on twenty-four hours a day and could only be controlled by one thing—to have Slow Larkin in her arms.

"Mother—"

Glorianna waved her beringed hand. "Put on some shorts and some flat-heeled shoes and stop arguing. You're coming."

Violet glared at her mother. And then she noticed Slow standing in the doorway to the pantry. He was fully dressed and sipping his first cup of coffee. His hair was wet; he must have just had his morning shower, too.

"She's right, Red," he said. "You've been working too hard. Come on with us, why don't you? Take a day just for fun."

Violet stared at him, all her hunger and unsatisfied desire probably written in her eyes for everyone to see. "I . . ." She found that somehow she'd lost the ability to say no to him. Probably because she'd been saying it for too long, when what she wanted to say was "Yes, all right. I'll come."

The words were out of her mouth before she perceived that she was actually saying them aloud.

Since Evan and the two Ferris girls jumped at the invitation, they needed two cars to accommodate them all. The children naturally wanted to ride with Slow in the Chevy. So the other three adults followed close behind in Arthur's comfortable sedan.

They arrived at the main gate on Exposition Boulevard just before eleven, having found parking spaces that seemed miles away. People streamed up the wide main road to the entrance, past the flags and the huge golden state bear.

Beyond the gate was the kid's fair, where Janine, Callie, Lacy and Evan painted their faces and left handprints in fingerpaint along with thousands of others on the walls. The exhibits were next, two levels and several huge buildings' full. The children became impatient by the time they reached the counties buildings and begged to head for the real action—the carnival midway.

Arthur volunteered to take them there, and then Glorianna decided to go, too. Slow was making arrangements to meet up with them in two hours before Violet even realized things were being contrived so that she and Slow would be alone. She opened her mouth to protest—and then shut it firmly.

They stood outside on the thoroughfare that ran between the two huge exhibit buildings. It was a hot, sunny day, and getting hotter. It would be sweltering on the midway, while the exhibit halls were cool.

And what could possibly happen between them while they milled and jostled with thousands of other weekend fairgoers? Beyond that, even if she could control herself no longer, and begged him to make love to her among the plastic grapes in the Napa County exhibit, they wouldn't be doing anything that they didn't both know they were going to do eventually anyway.

At that moment, as Slow looked over at her and smiled, something clicked inside Violet. Perhaps the time she'd needed to accept the inevitable had finally elapsed.

Whatever it was, she decided she was through with avoiding any situation where she might be caught alone with him. She was tired of running from her own desires. She wanted to be at his side today. To have fun with him as it seemed they'd never had time to have, back during their one short, passionate week years ago.

She reached out, grinning, and grabbed his hand, giggling under her breath at the way he stiffened at first in surprise, and then relaxed, his fingers entwining eagerly with her own. "All right," she said. "Come on, then." She gave the others a quick, warm glance. "We'll see you all in two hours." Then she pulled Slow through the double doors of the second building, which they had yet to tour.

Violet hardly even saw the rest of the counties' exhibits. The huge building, to her, was more an impression of light and sound, color and music than anything else. They stood, hand in hand before display after display, staring at animated papier mâché figures that grinned and danced among proud examples of the riches that each county produced. The crowds seemed to flow past them, full of laughter and excitement and impatience to see what came next.

When they'd toured the whole building, Slow led her out into the sun, announcing, "Next, my favorites."

"What?"

"The commercial exhibits. That's where you really get a show." He pulled her along, through the throngs, until he came to the building he sought.

Inside there were two stories of things to buy and the showmen who sold them. Violet stood beside Slow, her mouth hanging open in awe as a shammy salesman with a singsong Scandinavian accent brandished huge squares of what appeared to be yellow felt, announcing that "De shammy drinks de liquid," as he poured red-tinted water on a carpet sample, put the shammy down and gestured in satisfaction as the yellow felt seemed to suck up the red water. Then with a graceful flourish he wrung the shammy into a pitcher and began the process all over again.

Slow turned to Violet. "What do you think? Will your life be complete if you don't have one of those?"

Violet laughed, then pretended great gravity. "No, Slow. I don't think so. As a matter of fact, I have no idea how I've survived this long without a shammy of my own."

He nodded. "I understand." He turned to the salesman. "We'll take it." Slow handed over the money and was given a roll of yellow felt to tuck under his arm.

They proceeded to the next booth, where a fast-talking Easterner whipped gleaming kitchen knives around like a crazed ninja in a Bruce Lee movie. "They never need sharpening, folks. Guaranteed for life. *Your* life. And that's no lie..."

Slow bought Violet a set of knives. They wandered on to where a man who sounded fresh off the plantation demonstrated the incredible versatility of the Super-Duper-Slicer-Juicer. "It grates. It chops. It slices. It juices too. It makes yo' fancy cuts, and yo' simpluh cuts. Ladies, you all will wonder how in heaven you got by before you had yer very own Supe-ah-Dupe-ah-Slice-ah-Juice-ah!"

Slow looked at Violet, his blue eyes laughing, his face eager as a boy's. "Have you got to have that, or what?"

Violet glanced at the box of knives and the shammy roll he was already carrying. "Slow, let's not get carried away."

His lazy grin took her breath. "Aw, c'mon. Let's."

Violet swallowed, since her heart seemed to have somehow bounced into her throat. "We shouldn't," she said softly, talking about much more than the Super-Duper-Slicer-Juicer.

"Yeah, we should," he rejoined. "We should have what we want. Everything we want. After all this damn time. Haven't we waited long enough?"

Someone bumped against her from behind, pushing her closer to Slow. She found she didn't mind. She looked up at him, sighing, and then brushed his lips with her own, reveling in his quick, shallow intake of breath that told her how much the light caress meant to him.

"Yes," she said solemnly at last. "Buy me one of those, Slow. Buy me one of everything. Because that's what I want. Everything. After all these years."

"That's the way, little lady," intoned he salesman, holding out the Slicer-Juicer. "That'll be $34.98, and Ah'll throw in this minigrater at absolutely no chahge..."

After that they went from booth to booth, buying everything they saw—from a little broom in a case for quick cleanups in the car to a minimixer that whipped up diet shakes in a snap. Slow picked up fluorescent watches for the kids and several T-shirts, as well as a subscription to a new auto magazine and water-filled footpads for their shoes.

The buying spree ended only when neither of them could carry anymore. By some miracle they managed to secure huge shopping bags and then trekked all the way out to his car to get rid of the loot before meeting the others.

At the car, Violet hoisted her bag into the trunk after his and he neatly slammed the lid. Then she found herself facing him, there among the acres of automobiles beneath the burning afternoon sun. She was panting a little from carrying the big bag so far.

"Whew. That's my idea of a workout." She huffed. "Lugging the loot out to the car after a serious shopping spree."

He gazed at her fondly. "Right. I noticed since I've been living with you how much time you spend on shopping and indulging yourself. Zilch."

"Is that a criticism?" she teased.

"Nope." He touched her face with the back of his fingers, a light, stroking caress that caused her slowing heart to kick into high gear again. "I admire the hell out of you, Red. You don't spend a lot of time on trivial stuff. But I don't think it would hurt you to have a little more fun in your life."

She caught his hand, opened his palm and placed her lips in the heart of it. "I'm having fun now. Thanks to you."

His hand got away from her. It captured her chin. "A kiss?" His voice was low and rough, and he was so close that their lips were almost joined.

"Yes." She spoke the single word with husky eagerness. "Yes. One kiss. And then we'll have to run to get to the meeting place on time..."

His mouth touched hers. The sun blazed down on them, and some kid walking by let loose with a catcall, but Slow and Violet didn't care one bit. They tasted each other, their bodies pressed close, in a totally unhurried fashion.

At last Slow raised his head. "Tonight?" The question, though a little husky, was not a plea. He simply wanted to know if the languid kiss meant what he thought it had meant.

Violet looked at him and thought of the long, dry years she'd been without him. First the army had taken him from her, and then later she'd *sent* him away because...

Why, exactly? In the blinding light of this August afternoon, she could see more than one answer to that painful question.

Eleven years ago her mother had just left her father, and Glorianna had sworn she would never return to be stifled by the overbearing Clovis. In the end, when Clovis became ill, Glorianna *had* returned. But at the time, Violet's safe world had seemed torn apart. She couldn't bear to see her father hurt anymore. So when he'd burst in on her and Slow, she'd meekly gone with him rather than stand beside the man she loved.

And beyond misguidedly trying to protect her father from more hurt, she'd also secretly feared that she and Slow would end up like Glorianna and Clovis—too different to ever agree on anything, making each other miserable, bringing each other unhappiness instead of joy.

Worst of all, she hadn't been sure how they would live, since he had no money of his own and neither did she. She hadn't believed him when he swore they'd find a way.

Slow was looking at her tenderly now, his eyes hopeful but a little wary.

She had promised, years ago, to love him and stand beside him. And though it tore both of their hearts out, she had sent him away. That was her guilt and her shame.

Over a week ago, she had told another man she would wait to follow her heart until that other man returned. It occurred to her that she was behaving misguidedly again, cleaving to an unfair promise now, when she'd broken her heart's vow all those years ago.

The first promise was the true one, a voice whispered in her head. And a light dawned.

She was the most fortunate of women, in reality. For fate had given her one last chance to mend a vow she never should have broken.

She laid her hand on Slow's chest and felt the quickened rhythm of his heart against her palm.

"Yes, tonight, Slow," she said quietly, her eyes burning into his. "Please make love with me tonight."

Chapter Fifteen

For the rest of the day there was magic in everything.

Janine got a minor case of indigestion from an excess of pink popcorn and sat on a bench beneath the parachute roof of the California Country Stage, holding her stomach and moaning. Violet sat beside her, rubbing her back and whispering soothing words until the queasy feelings passed, finally taking Janine's head in her lap and stroking her curly hair back from her forehead.

She glanced up, to the picnic table nearby, where Evan and Lacy were pelting each other with peanut shells, Callie napped with her head on the table and Arthur and Glorianna held hands and swayed their shoulders in rhythm to the band on the stage. Slow was on the far side of the table, facing away toward the band.

Violet stared at his profile for a moment, thinking how wonderful the world was, here beneath the parachute canopy where it was only one hundred and five degrees instead of one hundred and ten like it was out in the sun, thinking that she could sit here forever, with a groaning child in her lap and two other kids screaming and yelling a few feet away, and a little country music for accompaniment.

Slow glanced back, as if he felt her eyes on him, and winked at her.

Pure magic, she thought, winking back.

After a while, Janine decided she had recovered sufficiently to go check out the petting zoo. They all went together into the big building that smelled of hay and warm, furry things. Violet did some petting herself, stroking the shorthaired, sleek coat of a white goat and a couple of furry guinea pigs—which she learned were more properly called cavies—as well as a tiny gray mouse whose little pink claws tickled her palms.

They moved on after that to the livestock barns, and the Hall of Flowers, and the California Forest Center, where they wandered the nature trails through the verdant examples of native trees of California and received a lesson about the renewable forest industry.

A three-acre attraction known as the Farm drew them next. There they oohed and ahhed over the hydroponic display, where crops were grown without soil, and Slow got into a long discussion with a crusty old character who collected and rebuilt miniature farm machinery as a hobby.

Of course they took their time touring Trans-Expo, where there were several mint-condition vintage cars.

"Glory, I think this model-A is older than you," Lacy remarked in awe.

The usually speechless Arthur spoke up then. "But nowhere near as beautiful," he said.

Even the sunset, when it came, was magical. A few clouds had drifted in as the afternoon passed. Wispy clouds and fleecy clouds, too. Things of fragile beauty, promising no rain at all. As the sun dropped beneath them, their undersides lit up, hot orange, in swirls and puffs.

"Magical," Violet breathed aloud and felt Slow's arm settle on the curve of her waist.

"Ain't that the truth," he confirmed and bent to nuzzle her neck. They stood near the huge fountain in the center of the fair, and right then a gust of wind blew the high jet of water toward them. They were misted with fountain spray. Around them, children, likewise sprayed, squealed in delighted protest.

"I wanna go to WaterWorld," Lacy begged from nearby.

"All right, all right." Slow laughed.

They all trooped over to WaterWorld, U.S.A., where they got drenched in the wave pool and slid down the Cliffhanger.

By nine, as true darkness came on, the kids really began to droop. It didn't appear as if they'd last until the closing fireworks display.

Glorianna took Violet aside. "We'll take the children home. You two stay. I'll ask Lacy Jay right now if she'd like to spend the night with me." Violet looked quickly up and away, overhead to where the sky tram was gliding by. She felt herself blushing, realizing how obvious she and Slow must have been. Then her mother's soft hand brushed her cheek. "Or am I presuming?'' Glorianna's voice was uncharacteristically mild.

Violet looked at her mother and smiled. "No, you're not. But ask Slow first, about Lacy."

Glorianna's eyes brimmed, but her smile was wide. "Are you happy, my love?"

"Yes, yes, I am."

"Then so am I, happy for you."

"Funny," Violet marveled. "I would have imagined, if I'd thought about it, that you would be gloating a little right now. I mean, since you've been right all these years."

Glorianna sighed. "No, I only wanted your happiness. That's really all most mothers want. Though perhaps we sometimes forget that our children have to find their own way—no matter how easy we could make it for them . . . if they'd only do as we say."

"I love you, Mother," Violet said.

"And I love you." Glorianna cupped Violet's chin in her hands and placed a kiss, like a soft benediction, on her forehead right above her nose. "I'll talk to Slow now," she said then and made her way over to where he sat with Arthur and the four children on a nearby stone bench.

Moments later Violet and Slow waved goodbye to the others as they left through the main gate.

Then Slow turned to her. "Are you ready?" he challenged.

"For what?" She laughed.

"The midway, of course. I'm going to win you a panda bear and kiss you in the Tunnel of Love."

He turned, pulling her behind, and forged through the crowds past the Expo Center and the children's carnival to the main midway, which, now that it was dark, glittered with a thousand lights.

The teeming crowds pushed and shoved around them, and the night was hot, the lights glaringly bright. The air smelled of cigarettes and corn dogs, drugstore perfume and sweat. Barkers called out their rough dares: "Knock 'em all down, you win the toy of your choice! Come on, mister, show your lady what you're made of! Fifty cents, and you could have it all..."

"Pure magic," Violet murmured and reached up to nibble Slow's ear.

They spun on the Tilt-a-World, and crashed into each other in bumper cars. Slow tossed quarters on plates and at last, after spending at least as much as the thing was worth, won her a huge yellow unicorn with a slightly crooked horn.

The carny taking tickets outside the Tunnel of Love wished Slow good luck when they snuggled together into the little car.

In the slightly cooler total darkness beyond the tunnel's entrance, Slow kissed her just as he'd promised and it was enchanting and funny and exciting all at once.

The little "car of love" moved along on its tracks, and some old love ballad played in the background as they rolled toward the midway lights once more.

They emerged, laughing, to find that the final event of the day—the fireworks display—was under way across the fairground at the grandstand. They didn't even try to make their way there.

Instead they stood, their arms around each other, beside a Dunk the Clown booth, and watched the star bursts and rockets light up the sky.

When it was over, Slow looked down at her. "Home now?" he asked.

She nodded and they turned for the main gate.

In the car, she snuggled against him, resting her hand on his thigh and recalling, unbidden, the few sweet times she'd ridden beside him like this all those years ago.

It seemed like no time at all before they were pulling up in front of the big, old house on East Broad Street. They got out and went to the trunk and, loaded down with all their crazy purchases, they stumbled up the front walk.

They were barely in the door before Slow was kissing her, and she was kissing him back, pressing herself up against him, offering her lips and her body—offering everything she had, without reservation.

He pulled her tight against him, his mouth locked on hers, and both of them groaned, hungry and full of sensual glee. He walked her backward—she tripped over her unicorn, and they both laughed into each other's mouths—until she came up against the arch to the living room.

There he lifted his mouth just enough to slant it the other way, making a soft growling sound in his throat. His hips ground against hers and her body answered his movements eagerly, with no holding back.

His mouth went exploring as he pinned her willing length against the arch. He nibbled her cheekbones, her temples, raising both hands to smooth back her hair and softly touch her face.

"You aren't wearing your glasses..." he noted in a tone of husky regret.

"No," she breathed back. "But I'll still do all those things you like, just as if I had been..."

He laughed, a low sound, and her feminine chuckle echoed it back.

She wore big round pink earrings, on clips, that matched her shorts and shirt. He caught one in his teeth and tugged it off, transferring it quickly to his hand.

"Poor little earlobe," he soothed as he very gently nipped it between his lips, "pinched all day like that." Violet let her head fall back against the arch, sighing as his lips and tongue massaged the tender skin of her lobe. At the same time, his hand was on her other ear, freeing it of its clip. He kneaded that lobe between his fingers.

Violet groaned and clutched his back, her senses stunned by how luxurious it felt. Such a tiny thing, removing her earrings and rubbing the circulation back into the tender skin beneath them, but so incredibly erotic because it showed such intimate knowledge of her body—what she felt and needed, even if she herself hadn't noticed the discomfort until he found it and massaged it away.

His lips slid down, over her exposed throat, kissing, tasting as they went. Her shirt had a boat neck so he nibbled out toward her shoulder, nipping and licking the taut skin over her collarbone.

Meanwhile, his hands were not idle. They glided, weightless as air over her breasts, which thrust out in instant invitation. He stroked them, the touch teasing and light, as she moved to offer them up, her body begging for more.

"Soon, Red, soon..." he muttered, teasing and soothing at the same time. She sought and found his mouth, kissing him wildly, hungry for his taste.

His hands left their delicate torment of her breasts then. They found the hem of her shirt, worked it free of her shorts and tugged upward. She raised her arms and he pulled the shirt over her head, tossing it to the floor with one hand while he held her two wrists high against the arch with the other.

He stroked her body. Long, slow strokes, soothing and arousing the tender inner surface of her upraised arms, gliding tauntingly over the plain cotton fabric of her bra, grasping for a moment the white skin over her ribs, which vibrated in and out with each agitated breath she took.

And then his hand worked at her belt. She heard the tiny growl of a zipper parting and felt him sliding her shorts over the curve of her hips with one hand. She wriggled, eager and impatient, until they slid down to her feet. Her arms still anchored high against the arch, she kicked her shorts away and then her slip-on pink flats. The shoes flew out, one hitting the front door, the other clanging against a brass planter in the corner.

He chuckled against her mouth. "In a hurry, are you?"

"Yes, and hungry..."

"For what?"

"For you..."

He pulled back enough to look into her eyes. "Say that again."

She whimpered a little, thrusting her body toward him. "Slow, please don't stop..."

"Say it. Say you want me."

His grip on her upraised arms had loosened. She gave a small tug and he released her. She reached for him, pulling him close, stroking his hair, reveling in the feel of rough denim against the bare skin of her exposed legs, against the thin shield of her panties, which were all that covered her womanhood now.

"Yes, yes, I want you," she crooned, pushing herself against him, cradling him at the same time. "I've always wanted you, and it's been a long, lonely time without you..."

He made a ragged sound and his arms clutched at her, forcing the breath from her as he held her. It was as if by squeezing her tightly the impossible might happen: they'd recover what they'd lost forever— eleven years they hadn't shared.

And then he pulled away again, bracing one hand on the frame of the arch behind her, and he slipped the other beneath the elastic waist of her plain cotton panties.

She quivered, and she stared at him, her mouth parted, her breath coming in short, sharp gasps. "Oh, Slow..."

His hand found her, parting her, his fingers slipping inside. "Move for me, show me," he commanded in a raspy whisper. "Show me how much you want me..." And he smiled, his eyes hot with knowing as he felt the liquid evidence of her readiness for him.

A long moan escaped her. She let her head, which now weighed too much for her neck to support, fall back against the arch as his fingers worked their magic in a deep, stroking rhythm, and she moved her hips eagerly in abandoned response.

As her movements grew more insistent, and he felt her nearing the edge, he suddenly paused, cupping her as she cried in her throat in protest.

"Wait, baby. Soon, I promise..." he murmured as he stripped her panties down.

Blindly she clutched at him, her hands all over him, trying furtively to pull off his shirt and to work at the button placket of his jeans at the same time.

He soothed her. "Easy. We'll get to that. Later. Relax now. Let me..." He found the clasp of her bra and unhooked it, freeing her breasts and stripping that last fragment of clothing away from her.

She sobbed in erotic need, holding her breasts up, pushing against him, begging for the exploding ecstasy that would bring this fabulous torment to a shattering sweet end.

He stroked her again, from her neck, over her breasts, lingering there briefly to tease her nipples with the flat of his palm, and then tug on them, just the slightest bit, until she moaned and writhed in ever-growing need.

His stroking touch proceeded downward, over her pale belly, which jerked and shuddered convulsively under his hand. And then he was touching her even lower down, his hand finding the heart of her need once more, two fingers sliding in and out, in a promise and a mimicry of the full mating to come.

Her mouth, gasping, sought his. And he gave her that, for a moment, his tongue stroking the delicate moistness beyond her lips.

And then he said against her mouth, "I want the taste of you..."

And she felt as if her knees couldn't possibly hold her upright until he'd had the taste he craved. He moved more fully in front of her, and then he slowly sank to his knees before her.

He parted her with his hands, and then he put his mouth there, his tongue delving in, laving what was already drenched with need.

Violet threw back her head and moaned at the ceiling as he took the round globes of her buttocks in his hands and brought her body even closer to his pleasuring mouth. Her hands seized his head, her fingers splayed in his hair, holding him to her as he brought her to the brink.

And at last it came, a rising, heated roll. A wave of liquid fire that picked her up and snapped, like a whip, lashing her out and over so she felt she tumbled, shuddering, quaking, screaming in ecstasy, calling his name.

After that there was a pure silence, and then the sound of rough breathing. And then Slow's eyes, in the heavy dimness of the entrance hall, looking up at her, heavy with shared satisfaction and the promise of more to come.

"I felt it," he said raggedly. "I felt it when it happened for you..."

Her hands, which had gone limp sometime while ecstasy took her, now cupped his head again. She pulled him, slowly, upright, reveling in the drugging, rough slide of his clothed body against her nude one.

She kissed him, tasting herself on his lips, and licking them, nipping them, thinking with a voluptuous sigh that the night was just beginning.

He laughed as she began working at the front of his jeans, and then he groaned as she put her hand there and lightly cupped his arousal.

"I'm naked," she whispered.

"I noticed," he growled.

"And you're not." She began slipping the metal buttons from their holes, pausing more than once to brush his clothed hardness as she worked to remove what kept it from her. Soon enough, she had all the buttons down.

He wore no underwear beneath, and she touched the silky length of him at last, pleasured by the way he jerked and groaned in response. She worked busily to push his jeans over his lean hips but then realized that he still wore his boots.

She knelt and removed them and his socks, glancing up every now and then, smiling, and then bending back to her work. At last his feet were bare and she rose again and pushed the jeans down. He shucked them off when they hit the floor.

"Now the shirt," she said, gathering it, raising it. "Lift your arms." He did, and she pulled it over his head and tossed it away. It landed on the banister, but neither of them really noticed.

"That's better." She sighed, her gaze caressing him all over, as his caressed hers.

"Yeah," he agreed. "Much better."

She put her hands on his sides, feeling the strong bones and sinews, and then she brought them around, as she'd dreamed in recent endless lonely nights of doing, to curl in the trail of hair down his belly. She nuzzled his chest as he clutched her head and moaned, and found his small nipples. She bit them, lightly, and he bucked against her in response.

Then, very slowly, as he had done, she knelt before him and tasted him, loving him as he had loved her, unrestrainedly, taking her pleasure from the hot explosion of his.

When that shattering intimacy was over, he cupped her face in his hands and guided her upright. "I need to lie down," he said. "To recover from that."

"My room," she instructed breathlessly.

He caught her beneath the knees and swung her up against his chest. He carried her from the hallway.

Neither of them looked back at what was left behind. At the strewn tangle of their clothes, or at the brimming shopping bags falling over, spilling their bounty by the door. Or at the yellow unicorn, on its side between the hall and the living room, its sightless eyes staring widely, its sewn-on mouth smiling and its horn pointing crookedly in the direction they had gone.

Chapter Sixteen

Violet left him briefly when they reached her room.

In the bathroom, she removed her contact lenses. Then she peered at her flushed face in the mirror. She was considering the possibility of not doing what she'd really come in here to do. She was thinking of leaving the little contraceptive device in its case.

She was past thirty, and she longed for children— Slow's children—no matter what happened in the end between the two of them. And, of course, now she knew that it was never going to be possible for her to marry Darrell.

That marriage, she realized now, had been her father's dream. And it was at last painfully clear that she had spent too many years virtually letting Clovis Windemere run her life. But that was over at last.

She held her destiny now in her own two hands. And never again would any other person wrest it from her.

However, owning her own destiny also meant respecting the destinies of others. And it would be wrong, she decided, to take a chance that they might create a child without having first discussed it with Slow.

Violet opened the medicine cabinet and removed the little case. A knock came at the door.

"Red? You okay?"

"Yes. Be right out." She quickly took the necessary measures to protect herself from pregnancy.

Slow was waiting for her on her bed. He held out his arms to her and she went eagerly into them. He kissed her, deeply, and the magic began anew.

His hands moved over her, readying her again, and she writhed and moaned and gave herself up without reluctance. His mouth closed on a breast, sucking strongly, and she clutched his head, holding herself arched for him so he could drink in her sweetness. He bit her lightly and sucked even more strongly, and she pleaded with him, inchoately, never, ever, to let it end.

His roving hands discovered all her secrets. She gave them up willingly, offering them as grateful tributes for the pleasure that he brought.

He touched her intimately again and found her ready as he knew she'd be. And then he levered himself up on an arm, his fingers still casting their spell, his eyes willing her to look at him.

When she forced her heavy lids to part, he said, "Now, Red? Do you want it to be now?"

Her long, hungry sigh told him everything. He nudged her legs apart and moved between them. She opened for him, like a new rose for the heat of the sun. He pushed into her; she whimpered and hungrily raised her hips, offering herself fully.

He took what she offered, gliding deep into her, making a low sound as her softness closed around him.

She bucked against him, he held her steady, and then he began to move. At first she lay there, unmoving herself but totally receptive, her pale face transfixed with a kind of erotic awe.

Slow looked down at her, sheathed at last within her as he'd longed to be, forever, it seemed. He thought that she was everything, in the way she gave and the way she took. He thought he would die from the pleasure of her tight sweetness all around him. And he thought it would be a great way to go.

He slid out of her, tantalizingly, and back in once more, over and over. Her eyelids, heavy with her building passion, drooped closed.

She moaned. He speeded up the rhythm.

She raised her legs to lock around him and she clutched his back, meeting and matching his every thrust.

They rolled in a wild, hungry tangle until they were facing each other on their sides and they stayed like that, locked together, moving deeply and fully as one.

The wave of fulfillment rose once more, this time for both of them.

Violet felt it rising first, swelling to a massive, high fullness, and then breaking against the place where they were joined, shattering the entire universe in a shower of liquid flame.

Slow's satisfaction came right after hers as he felt her delicate inner muscles tighten around him, milking him, taking all he had to give and giving it right back to him.

He thrust deeply into her, and she took him. It felt as if she suddenly opened wide, and then closed around him, so that he tumbled over the brink, pulsing into her, his head thrown back, his throat opened in a long, deep masculine cry of triumph and utter capitulation at one and the same time.

They lay together, still entwined, for a long while after that, idly touching and stroking whenever the urge struck. Violet smiled, remembering that they had lain like this all those years ago, and she had kept him within her so they could start all over again.

She wondered, as her fingers combed the hair at his temples, what it would be like to lie wrapped up with him like this for all the remaining nights of their lives. She thought that she'd certainly like to find out. And that they would have to talk about that. About the future. Soon, very soon.

But not tonight, she thought. Tonight wasn't for talking. Tonight was for touching and kissing and stroking. Tonight was for making love.

"What are you smiling about?" he asked huskily.

"Just thinking. About tonight."

"What about tonight?"

"That it's for making love," she told him.

He grinned in response to that, and then he pulled her even closer, lowering his head so that he could nuzzle her breasts. His mouth closed over the taut bud of a nipple. Violet moaned and gave herself over to the shimmering pleasure only Slow's touch could bring.

* * *

The next morning Violet woke rather late for the early riser she was. The clock by the bed said almost nine.

She smiled, a smile of pure fulfillment, and lay very still for a time within the cherishing cradle of Slow's arms. He felt so warm, all wrapped around her. His even breathing stirred her hair.

She wriggled a little so she could turn over and see him. He made a grunting sound of protest in his sleep, tensing, as if he dreamed she was trying to leave him and thought to hold her there. But then he relaxed, and she turned and looked at him.

He looked so vulnerable in sleep, his mouth soft, his forehead smooth.

"I love you, Slow Larkin," she whispered, not loud enough to wake him. "I love you." She said it again, kind of trying it out, rehearsing it for when she would tell him later, after she'd gotten some breakfast in him and they were both fully awake.

She was nervous about telling him because she had said she loved him once before, long ago, and then had sent him from her life. She was a little afraid that he simply wouldn't believe her now, or that he would reject her, the way she'd rejected him before.

But, she told herself firmly, nothing ventured . . .

She decided she would fix breakfast and then wake him. He hated to be wakened too early, of course. But she had a feeling that he might make an exception in this case. Glorianna would be bringing Lacy home by noon or so, and she wanted things out in the open between them before then.

Carefully, so as not to wake him, Violet slipped out from under his arm. She put on her glasses, found her slippers and then tiptoed to the bathroom. She started to shower but then didn't. His scent and the scent of their lovemaking was all around her. She decided to let it linger for a while, smiling a feminine smile as she imagined they might shower together later, if there was time before Lacy returned.

After rinsing her face and quickly running a comb through her hair, she threw on the robe that hung on a peg behind the door and went into the kitchen. Within minutes the kitchen smelled of frying bacon and brewing coffee.

She cracked several eggs in a bowl and whipped them up, grinning when she realized that she had yet to learn how Slow liked his eggs. She made toast and squeezed some oranges of their sweet pulpy juice, and then finally arranged two plates on a big tray that she found in the butler's pantry.

When the fluffy eggs were done and the coffee brewed, she filled the plates, balanced the tray in one hand and hefted the coffeepot in the other. She took a step toward the door to her bedroom.

And the doorbell rang.

Violet winced and set the tray and coffeepot down. Lacy Jay was home much sooner than expected. She considered the situation and then decided there was nothing to do but go open the door.

She was through the butler's pantry and passing the stairs in the hall before it occurred to her that Lacy had a key and wouldn't be ringing the bell anyway.

Then she noticed the state of the entrance hall—with the tumble of packages from the fair piled by the door, and her and Slow's clothes strewn all over. Her face turned pink because it looked exactly like what it was—the place where two eager lovers had gotten rid of the hindrance of their clothes.

The door chimes rang again. Violet looked at the door itself then. Through the etched glass panes at the top, she could make out the shape of a man.

The shape looked familiar.

And then it hit her.

"Darrell." She breathed the word in horrified disbelief.

He rang the doorbell again, impatiently, and she could see him trying to peer through the etched panes into the dimness where she stood.

She didn't move for agonized seconds more because this wasn't the way she had wanted him to learn that whatever he hoped for between them could never be.

But then she drew herself up. It had to happen, one way or another, she told herself. She'd simply have to make the best of the way it was.

Quickly, as he punched the doorbell again, she flew about gathering up the strewn clothes, thinking only that she could at least spare Darrell the blatant evidence of what had happened here.

It never occurred to her that the continuing ringing of the bell might have wakened Slow, or how guilty and furtive she would look, scurrying about grabbing up their clothes in a frantic effort to hide them from Darrell.

"Strange time to clean house," a voice said from the door to the butler's pantry behind her.

Violet whirled, clutching the pile of clothes against her chest. "Oh! Slow, you scared me."

"You look guilty as hell, Red." His eyes were hooded. He was totally nude. "What's going on?"

She glanced hopelessly at the door. "It's . . ."

"Violet!" Darrell knocked sharply. "Violet, are you there?"

"It's Darrell," Violet finished lamely.

Slow looked from the wad of clothing in her arms to her agonized face and then back at the door. "I see that. And I think you're going to have to let him in."

"But I . . ."

"You what?"

"Violet!" Darrell knocked and called again.

"I feel awful, having him see . . ."

Slow held out his hands. "All right. Give those here." She numbly handed the pile over to him. After extricating his jeans, he spun and threw the rest in a corner of the pantry behind him. Then he shoved his legs into the jeans and quickly buttoned them up. "Now. Answer the door."

The short hall seemed to go on forever, but Violet at last made it to the door. She pulled it open just as Darrell was raising his fist to knock once more.

His frown dissolved into a huge smile. "Darling."

"Darrell." Violet tried to force a smile. "What in the world—"

He rushed to explain. "I just got in. Drove all night again. I'm here till Tuesday to make all the arrangements for Mom and Dad. Then I'll fly back to get them Tuesday night."

"But you never—"

He cut her off again. "I called yesterday," he said quickly. "I left a message on your machine."

"Oh, I see," Violet said weakly. The last thing on her mind the night before had been checking her messages.

"Did I wake you?" Darrell asked, all solicitude. "I'm sorry, but I . . ." His eyes narrowed as he began to register her flushed face and her strained expression. "I couldn't wait to see you," he finished on a flat note. Then, "Violet, what is it?"

Violet swallowed, and then she forced herself to speak in a calm, level voice. "Come in, Darrell. There's . . . something we need to talk about."

Suddenly his pale eyes slid away, and Violet realized that Darrell didn't really want to know what she intended to tell him. He said, "Wait a minute, perhaps it would be better if—"

Violet put up a hand. "No, Darrell. We need to get this out in the open now." She stood back, fully opening the door. And Darrell and Slow faced each other down the short length of the hall.

"'Lo, Darrell," Slow said in his laziest drawl.

Darrell glared at Slow. "What is this?" he demanded on an indrawn breath. And then he looked at Violet, at her flushed face and thin robe, and then back once more at Slow, who resembled nothing so much as the tousled bed he'd just risen from.

"Darrell," Violet tried carefully. "Please come in, and we'll discuss—"

He cut her off with a short, chopping movement of his hand. He wasn't even looking at Violet, his furious gaze was focused on his lifelong rival across the hall.

"You bastard," Darrell said in an ugly voice. "You did it, didn't you? Just as you said you would."

Violet blinked, confused. "Did what?" she asked, turning to Slow. For a moment she saw pure pain and self-disgust on his face, but then he looked away. Hurting for him, though she didn't even know what had wounded him, she took a step in his direction. "Slow? What is it? What's wrong?"

"I'll tell you what's wrong," Darrell cut into the silence almost gleefully. "He came back to get even, Violet, for things that happened years and years ago. He came back to—" he faltered over the word "—seduce you, for revenge on me because I love you. And he's done what he came back for, I can see. He's had his disgusting revenge."

Violet was still staring at Slow. "Slow?" she asked, bewildered, "what is he talking about?"

Slow looked at her. The anguish she saw in his eyes made her ache for him. She wanted to go to him, put her arms around him, tell him that, whatever it was, it would be all right. But when she lifted her arms, he stiffened, warding her off with every line of his lean frame, pulling aloneness around his bare shoulders like a cloak.

"Slow?" This time there was a pleading note in her voice.

"As you can see, I'm telling the truth," Darrell stiffly intoned from behind her. "And now, Violet, I would like to speak with you alone. I have quite a lot to say to you."

Violet felt, right then, an eerie shudder skitter along her skin. It was eleven years later, everything had changed. Now it was Darrell rather than her father ordering her to forsake the man she loved. But still the moment had come. Again. She was being given, as she'd realized yesterday, another chance to mend the vow once wrongly broken.

She sent a brief prayer to heaven. *Please God, let me do it right this time...*

She said softly to Slow. "I think I'd better go with him."

Slow winced, as if the words hurt him. But then he nodded. "Yeah, I understand." His voice was very controlled.

She turned to Darrell. "Please wait in your car. I'll be dressed in a minute."

"All right," Darrell said grudgingly. "But hurry."

"I will."

Chapter Seventeen

There was a tiny park at the base of Commercial Street, tucked between a gas station and an antique store. Violet had Darrell take her there to talk.

They sat together on a brick planter beneath the trees. The morning was warm, promising a hot day later on.

Darrell tried to take her hand.

"Now, Violet," he said gruffly when she rejected his touch. "It isn't the end of the world. We can work it out, I'm sure. With time, I will forgive you, and—"

She didn't let him go on. "*When* exactly did Slow tell you about this revenge of his?"

He cleared his throat. "Now, darling, none of that matters now. It's over and the wisest thing to do is—"

"Answer my question, Darrell."

He huffed a little more. And then he confessed. "All right. The Monday after he arrived. I sought him out alone."

"Even though I asked you several times not to do that? Even though you specifically told me you wouldn't?"

He looked away, took a breath and then looked back at her. "All right. I was wrong. We *both* have been wrong. Now we need to start making things right."

"Exactly," she agreed. "So please tell me now what you did years and years ago that would make Slow want to take revenge on you now."

Darrell blinked. "What? Violet I haven't the faintest idea what you are talking about."

"You said Slow came back to get even, for *things* that happened years ago."

He coughed again. "Well, I meant the way you... broke up with him. I meant he wanted revenge for that."

"But you said he was taking revenge to get even with *you,* Darrell."

"I—"

"Darrell, I want the truth. I want all of the truth. I think it's about time."

"Violet, he was always bad for you," Darrell argued in an agonized voice. "Whatever I did, I did it for you."

"I want the truth, Darrell. Is that so much to ask?"

Darrell stood. He walked to the edge of the little cobbled walk and stared into the tangle of trees. Then he glanced up at the sky. Violet waited, until he finally turned around.

He said, "You're never going to marry me, are you? No matter how much I love you, you just don't love me back."

She looked at him without wavering. "No, Darrell. I don't. I'm beginning to think I don't even *like* you much, if you want the brutal truth."

He said, "You're going away with him, aren't you?" His voice was bleak.

"That's between Slow and me. But whatever happens, you and I are through."

He made one last pleading attempt. "Damn it, Violet, what about the firm? What about our fathers' dreams for us?"

"I'll clear my calendar in the next week and we'll dissolve the partnership," she said evenly, knowing it was the right thing to do.

"But what will I do without you, now of all times? How will I handle both your work load and mine, when I have two unwell parents to think about."

She looked at him levelly and kept her voice firm. "We have to make the break, Darrell. And there would always be some excuse not to. So it's going to be now. I won't draw it out any longer."

His face turned hard. "You're making the biggest mistake of your life."

"I think you're wrong. But even if you aren't, at least it'll be my *own* mistake." She stood. "And now, are you going to tell me why Slow wanted revenge?"

Darrell grunted. "What for? Ask him. He'll be glad to tell you, I'm sure."

"All right, Darrell," Violet said, "that's exactly what I'll do."

Violet left Darrell at the park and used the uphill walk past the shops of Commercial Street to clear her mind for the confrontation with Slow that lay ahead of her.

She kept thinking of the bleak agony in his blue eyes when he'd told her to go ahead and leave with Darrell. It was going to be a battle, she knew, to get him to share his pain with her, and to get to the bottom of the mysteries, both past and present.

The house seemed preternaturally quiet when Violet let herself in. As she closed the front door behind her, her gaze fell on the yellow unicorn, still lying on its side beneath the arch to the living room. She smiled to herself and picked it up, rubbing her cheek against its soft fur.

Then, still idly petting the soft trophy he'd won for her the night before, she wandered through the pantry, the empty kitchen where their now cold breakfast still waited on the counter and into her room. He wasn't there. She returned to the entrance hall, and then slowly mounted the stairs.

She found him in her father's room, shoving clothes into his black duffel bags. She leaned against the arch, watching him, petting the toy unicorn, wondering where to begin.

He became aware of her before she spoke and said, in a strained mockery of his usual insolent drawl, "As soon as Lacy gets back, we'll get out of your hair."

The fact that he was actually taking steps to leave her pierced her to the heart. Her eyes brimmed with tears. She forced them back. It was not a time for tears. It was a time to be strong, as she hadn't been years ago.

She had to remember that she had rejected him once, totally, in similar circumstances. She had to remember how hard it had been for him, all those years ago, a boy without a mother, whose father had virtually disowned him. The risk to his heart and soul in loving her then had been great, yet he had taken it. Only to lose all.

She wouldn't have imagined he'd ever have been bold—or foolish—enough to take that risk again. Yet he *had* come back finally. And pursued her. And won her.

And now they'd come full circle. They stood at the moment of choice once more. She couldn't blame him in the least for wanting to salvage some scrap of pride for himself—to leave before, as he presumed, she could kick him out.

It would be up to her to make him see otherwise. That was why she couldn't afford the indulgence of a tearful scene.

She went on petting the unicorn. "And where are you headed this time?" she asked when she was sure her voice wouldn't waver.

He attempted a lazy shrug. "Someplace where I can get a decent burger at 3:00 a.m. Back to North Hollywood, I guess. Lacy Jay'll like that. She's done fine here, but she misses her weird friends. And you were right about that garage. It would have been like going backward. I've got some expansion plans in the works at Classic Cars, Incorporated. I think it's time I came back from vacation and saw my plans through."

"I understand," Violet said. She went on stroking the stuffed animal and it seemed she could feel his hot gaze on her. She looked up into his eyes.

"Who did I think I was kidding anyway?" he blurted in a voice gone suddenly raspy with pain. "This is a beautiful little town but it's never been the place for me."

"Then why did you come back?"

For a moment he just looked at her, his eyes burning through her. Then his lips curled in an ironic smile. "Because I'm one of those hopeless idiots who's just got to try one more time to get the girl." Violet's heart leaped at the words. But he had already turned away and resumed shoving clothes into bags.

"Slow?"

"What?"

"What happened all those years ago? Between you and Darrell?"

"It doesn't matter."

"Yes, it does," she said firmly. "It matters a lot. Three people were involved from the way I see it— you, me and Darrell. You two know the truth, whatever it was. And I've been kept in the dark. It isn't right. I deserve to know."

He dropped to the bed then and rubbed his eyes with his fingers. "All right."

She approached, cautiously, and sat down beside him. In a quiet voice he told her—of the truth behind the incident with the Corvette, that Darrell had tried to bribe him and then that he was reasonably sure Darrell had told Clovis that she and Slow were in love.

When he was finished, he stood immediately and busied himself yanking his things out of the closet once more. Violet watched him, thinking how it all made sense at last, and marveling that she hadn't suspected before.

But Slow had been right. It didn't matter now that she knew. There was little she could do about the past, it was over and gone. What mattered was right now.

Still she couldn't help admitting, "I wish I'd gone with you eleven years ago. I'm jealous of all that time that we didn't have together."

Slow froze at those words and turned from the closet to face her. "What are you saying?"

She smiled at him sadly. "That I was young and confused, and that my mother had left my father and I didn't want to see him hurt anymore. But I was a fool. Because I loved you then *almost* as much as I love you now."

He stared at her. And then he said in a voice that was more growl than anything else. "Do you mean this?"

She nodded. "I do. But you know—"

"What?"

"When I think about it, it's fine that everything happened just as it did. If I had gone with you then, there'd be no Lacy Jay. And I can't imagine a world without Lacy Jay."

She saw the hope flare in his eyes, and then she saw it flicker and fade. "Wait a minute," he said. "Look. You still don't get it. I'm no more of a prize than Darrell is. What he said was true. I purposely set out this time to get you into bed. I wanted revenge, not on him but on *you*. I wanted to make you want me so bad that you'd beg me to make love to you. I . . . I played you like a poker game, Red."

She smiled. "Yes. You certainly did."

"And you have every right to hate me now."

"Oh, do I?"

"Damn it, yes."

She stood, setting the unicorn aside. "I should hate you?"

"Hell, yes."

"For what?"

"You know what."

"For filling my house with life and laughter, for fixing everything in sight, for making me feel beautiful and desired? For sharing your child with me? Keeping dinner warm for me? For buying me the state fair and then loving me until I couldn't see straight?" She slowly approached him. "Gee whiz, Slow. If that's the way you take revenge on me, I have only one request to make..."

He backed toward the far wall as she relentlessly came on. "What?" he demanded warily.

She had him with his back to the wall. She pressed herself against him, glorying in the feel of him. "I want you to never, ever, stop...."

He looked into her eyes and at last allowed himself to see the desire and love burning there. "You're crazy," he muttered prayerfully.

"No," she said, laying her hands on his bare chest. "I'm saner than I've ever been. More *myself* than I ever imagined I could be."

He dared to ask then, "You'll come with me this time? *Marry* me this time?"

"I need a week to wrap things up for good with Windemere and Carruthers," she said. "And then, yes, anywhere you say. To the ends of the earth."

He grabbed for her, pulling her tight against him, burying his face in her hair. But then her glasses bumped his ear. He pulled back a little, daring to smile himself now. And very carefully he took her glasses off.

She said in a low purr, "You shouldn't have done that. We have so much more to say. We have to plan how we'll tell Lacy, and when exactly we'll get married, and if we'll need a new house in North Hollywood..."

He set her glasses on the mahogany bureau nearby and began working at the buttons of her shirt. "We'll tell Lacy and Glory as soon as they arrive. We'll get married tonight. In Reno, because now that I know you're with me, I want you with me for all the world to see. And my house in North Hollywood is huge, big enough for all those kids we want, but we can look for another one if you don't like it..." He peeled back her shirt and pushed it down her arms. Then he unclasped her bra.

"Slow..." She sighed. "The door...in case Lacy..."

He grabbed her hand, pulled her to the door, kicked it shut and turned the lock. "Anything else?"

"Well, I should probably put in my—"

He pulled her up against him. "Don't you want ten babies?"

"Yes, oh, yes. You know I do."

"Then I think it's time we got started on the first one, don't you?" He kissed her, but only briefly. Then he lifted his head enough to say, "I love you, Violet Anne Windemere."

"And I love you, Winslow Larkin," she solemnly told him in reply.

Then at last he kissed her, a *real* kiss that set her body aflame and curled her toes inside her shoes. Violet wrapped her arms around him and kissed him right back, grateful beyond measure to have been on the receiving end of Slow Larkin's special brand of revenge.

* * * * *

COMING NEXT MONTH

#703 SOMEONE TO TALK TO—Marie Ferrarella
Lawyer Brendan Connery was dreading the long-overdue reunion
with his ailing father. But then nurse Shelby Tyree appeared by
Brendan's side, offering to help him heal the wounds of the past....

#704 ABOVE THE CLOUDS—Bevlyn Marshall
Renowned scientist discovers abominable snowman.... Was it genius
or madness? Laura Prescott sought to save her father's reputation;
newspaperman Steve Slater sensed a story. On their Himalayan hunt
for truth, would they find love instead?

#705 THE ICE PRINCESS—Lorraine Carroll
To DeShea Ballard, family meant pain; to Nick Couvillion, it meant a
full house and kisses on both cheeks. An orphaned nephew united
them, but could one man's fire melt an ice princess?

#706 HOME COURT ADVANTAGE—Andrea Edwards
Girls' basketball coach Jenna Lauren dropped her defenses once
boys' coach Rob Fagan came a-courting...again. Familiar hallways
harkened back to high school romance, but this time, love wasn't just
child's play....

#707 REBEL TO THE RESCUE—Kayla Daniels
Investigator Slade Marshall was supposed to discover why
Tory Clayton's French Quarter guest house lay smoldering in ashes.
Instead, he fanned the flames...of her heart.

#708 BABY, IT'S YOU—Celeste Hamilton
Policeman Andy Baskin and accountant Meg Hathaway shirked
tradition. They got married, divorced, then, ten years later, had a
child. But one tradition prevailed—everlasting love—beckoning
them home.

AVAILABLE THIS MONTH:

FASHION
A WHOLE NEW YOU
WIN
CARS, TRIPS, CASH!

SILHOUETTE®
OFFICIAL SWEEPSTAKES
RULES

NO PURCHASE NECESSARY

1. To enter, complete an Official Entry Form or 3" × 5" index card by hand-printing, in plain block letters, your complete name, address, phone number and age, and mailing it to: Silhouette Fashion A Whole New You Sweepstakes, P.O. Box 9056, Buffalo, NY 14269-9056.

   No responsibility is assumed for lost, late or misdirected mail. Entries must be sent separately with first class postage affixed, and be received no later than December 31, 1991 for eligibility.

2. Winners will be selected by D.L. Blair, Inc., an independent judging organization whose decisions are final, in random drawings to be held on January 30, 1992 in Blair, NE at 10:00 a.m. from among all eligible entries received.

3. The prizes to be awarded and their approximate retail values are as follows: Grand Prize — A brand-new Ford Explorer 4×4 plus a trip for two (2) to Hawaii, including round-trip air transportation, six (6) nights hotel accommodation, a $1,400 meal/spending money stipend and $2,000 cash toward a new fashion wardrobe (approximate value: $28,000) or $15,000 cash; two (2) Second Prizes — A trip to Hawaii, including round-trip air transportation, six (6) nights hotel accommodation, a $1,400 meal/spending money stipend and $2,000 cash toward a new fashion wardrobe (approximate value: $11,000) or $5,000 cash; three (3) Third Prizes — $2,000 cash toward a new fashion wardrobe. All prizes are valued in U.S. currency. Travel award air transportation is from the commercial airport nearest winner's home. Travel is subject to space and accommodation availability, and must be completed by June 30, 1993. Sweepstakes offer is open to residents of the U.S. and Canada who are 21 years of age or older as of December 31, 1991, except residents of Puerto Rico, employees and immediate family members of Torstar Corp., its affiliates, subsidiaries, and all agencies, entities and persons connected with the use, marketing, or conduct of this sweepstakes. All federal, state, provincial, municipal and local laws apply. Offer void wherever prohibited by law. Taxes and/or duties, applicable registration and licensing fees, are the sole responsibility of the winners. Any litigation within the province of Quebec respecting the conduct and awarding of a prize may be submitted to the Régie des loteries et courses du Québec. All prizes will be awarded; winners will be notified by mail. No substitution of prizes is permitted.

4. Potential winners must sign and return any required Affidavit of Eligibility/Release of Liability within 30 days of notification. In the event of noncompliance within this time period, the prize may be awarded to an alternate winner. Any prize or prize notification returned as undeliverable may result in the awarding of that prize to an alternate winner. By acceptance of their prize, winners consent to use of their names, photographs or their likenesses for purposes of advertising, trade and promotion on behalf of Torstar Corp. without further compensation. Canadian winners must correctly answer a time-limited arithmetical question in order to be awarded a prize.

5. For a list of winners (available after 3/31/92), send a separate stamped, self-addressed envelope to: Silhouette Fashion A Whole New You Sweepstakes, P.O. Box 4665, Blair, NE 68009.

PREMIUM OFFER TERMS

To receive your gift, complete the Offer Certificate according to directions. Be certain to enclose the required number of "Fashion A Whole New You" proofs of product purchase (which are found on the last page of every specially marked "Fashion A Whole New You" Silhouette or Harlequin romance novel). Requests must be received no later than December 31, 1991. Limit: four (4) gifts per name, family, group, organization or address. Items depicted are for illustrative purposes only and may not be exactly as shown. Please allow 6 to 8 weeks for receipt of order. Offer good while quantities of gifts last. In the event an ordered gift is no longer available, you will receive a free, previously unpublished Silhouette or Harlequin book for every proof of purchase you have submitted with your request, plus a refund of the postage and handling charge you have included. Offer good in the U.S. and Canada only.

SLFW-SWPR

SILHOUETTE® OFFICIAL SWEEPSTAKES ENTRY FORM

4-FWSES-3

Complete and return this Entry Form immediately – the more entries you submit, the better your chances of winning!

- Entries must be received by **December 31, 1991.**
- A Random draw will take place on **January 30, 1992.**
- No purchase necessary.

Yes, I want to win a FASHION A WHOLE NEW YOU Sensuous and Adventurous prize from Silhouette.

Name _____ Telephone _____ Age _____

Address _____

City _____ State _____ Zip _____

Return Entries to: **Silhouette FASHION A WHOLE NEW YOU,**
P.O. Box 9056, Buffalo, NY 14269-9056   © 1991 Harlequin Enterprises Limited

PREMIUM OFFER

To receive your free gift, send us the required number of proofs-of-purchase from any specially marked FASHION A WHOLE NEW YOU Silhouette or Harlequin Book with the Offer Certificate properly completed, plus a check or money order (do not send cash) to cover postage and handling payable to Silhouette FASHION A WHOLE NEW YOU Offer. We will send you the specified gift.

OFFER CERTIFICATE

Item	A. SENSUAL DESIGNER VANITY BOX COLLECTION (set of 4) (Suggested Retail Price $60.00)	B. ADVENTUROUS TRAVEL COSMETIC CASE SET (set of 3) (Suggested Retail Price $25.00)
# of proofs-of-purchase	18	12
Postage and Handling	$3.50	$2.95
Check one	☐	☐

Name _____

Address _____

City _____ State _____ Zip _____

Mail this certificate, designated number of proofs-of-purchase and check or money order for postage and handling to: **Silhouette FASHION A WHOLE NEW YOU Gift Offer,** P.O. Box 9057, Buffalo, NY 14269-9057. Requests must be received by December 31, 1991.

ONE PROOF-OF-PURCHASE   4-FWSEP-3

To collect your fabulous free gift you must include the necessary number of proofs-of-purchase with a properly completed Offer Certificate.

© 1991 Harlequin Enterprises Limited

See previous page for details.